Thoroughbred Legacy
The stakes are high.

Scandal has hit the Preston family and their award-winning Quest Stables. Find out what it will take to return this horse-racing dynasty to the winner's circle!

Available July 2008

#1 *Flirting with Trouble* by Elizabeth Bevarly
Publicist Marnie Roberts has just been handed a PR disaster, one that will bring her face-to-face with the man who walked out of her bed and out of her life eight years ago.

#2 *Biding Her Time* by Wendy Warren
Somehow, Audrey Griffin's motto of "seize the day" has unexpectedly thrown her into the arms of a straitlaced Aussie who doesn't do no-strings-attached. Is Audrey balking at commitment…or simply biding her time?

#3 *Picture of Perfection* by Kristin Gabriel
When Carter Phillips sees an exquisite painting that could be the key to saving his career, he goes after the artist. Will he sacrifice his professional future for a personal one with her?

#4 *Something to Talk About* by Joanne Rock
Widowed single mom Amanda Emory is on the run from her past, but when she meets Quest's trainer she suddenly wants to risk it all…and give everyone something to talk about!

Available September 2008
#5 *Millions To Spare* by Barbara Dunlop
#6 *Courting Disaster* by Kathleen O'Reilly
#7 *Who's Cheatin' Who?* by Maggie Price
#8 *A Lady's Luck* by Ken Casper

Available December 2008
#9 *Darci's Pride* by Jenna Mills
#10 *Breaking Free* by Loreth Anne White
#11 *An Indecent Proposal* by Margot Early
#12 *The Secret Heiress* by Bethany Campbell

Dear Reader,

As an animal-science major, I've always been fascinated by horses, so it was a thrill for me to write this third installment of the wonderful THOROUGHBRED LEGACY series.

There's something special about people who love animals, and veterinarian Carter Phillips is no exception. When he meets artist Gillian Cameron, she throws his life completely off track—especially when a dark secret threatens them both.

The world of Thoroughbred horse racing is full of exciting twists and turns, so hold on to your cowboy hat and enjoy the ride!

All my best,

Kristin Gabriel

Thoroughbred Legacy

PICTURE OF PERFECTION

Kristin Gabriel

Silhouette Books

Published by Silhouette Books

America's Publisher of Contemporary Romance

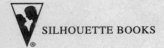

SILHOUETTE BOOKS

ISBN-13: 978-0-373-19916-7
ISBN-10:   0-373-19916-3

PICTURE OF PERFECTION

Special thanks and acknowledgment are given to Kristin Gabriel
for her contribution to the Thoroughbred Legacy series.

Visit Silhouette Special Edition and Thoroughbred Legacy
at www.eHarlequin.com.

Printed in U.S.A.

KRISTIN GABRIEL

is an author of more than twenty-five books.
She is a two-time Romance Writers of America
RITA® Award winner for best traditional romance.
Her first book was made into a television movie
entitled *Recipe for Revenge*. Kristin lives in rural
Nebraska, and her favorite hobbies are snacking and
procrastination.

For the awesome members
of Prairieland Romance Writers:

Sherry James, Julie Miller, Sue Baumann,
Mary Ann McQuillan, Kathleen Pieper,
Noelle Ptomey, Pam Crooks, Brenda Kranz,
Robin Rotham, Heidi Aken, Margaret Cowan McGrath,
Cindy Kirk, Elizabeth Parker, Yvonne Weers,
Patricia Riley and Ellen Ambroz.

Thank you for inspiring me, making me laugh
and making me a better writer.

Prologue

Smoke.

Thick and black, it blinded Gillian as she stumbled
toward the door, her arms outstretched to feel her way
along the wall of her bedroom. The smoke filled her
nostrils and throat, threatening to choke her. She tried
not to breathe it in as she sought escape, her eyes
burning and thick with tears.

Almost there.

She could hear glass breaking somewhere in the
ranch house and a strange rumbling beneath her feet.
There was only smoke and darkness in her second-
floor bedroom, no flames to light her way. She
imagined those hot flames licking the floor below her,

like a ravenous beast consuming everything in its path. The image frightened her, making her long for the comforting arms of her parents.

She tried to call out for them, but smoke filled her lungs as soon as she opened her mouth. Her cry was lost in a fit of coughing that made her chest ache. Surrounded by the smoky darkness, she felt a sense of hopelessness begin to seep into her veins, making her body feel so heavy that it was difficult to move.

Where was the door?

It took all her strength to extend her arms over the wall as she searched for the door frame. She felt as if she'd already walked several miles rather than just the few feet that led from her bed to the hallway.

Had she gone in the wrong direction?

No, surely not. It wasn't possible to get lost in your own bedroom, was it? She paused, indecision clogging her brain. She was so tired. She just wanted to lie down on her pink shag carpet and go to sleep again, but the desperate need for air kept pushing her forward.

Her next step landed on something small and soft. It emitted a mournful squeak as her foot pressed it against the floor. The sound came from Morris, her favorite teddy bear. Gillian bent down and snatched him up, reveling in the familiar feel of him. He was like a signpost in the night, telling her this dark, scary place really was her home.

She held the teddy bear tightly against her chest.

Gillian couldn't let Morris burn. She'd had him for ten years, ever since she was born. She had to save him.

She had to save her parents.

Gillian kept moving, her chest beginning to ache as she took short, shallow breaths to keep from inhaling too much of the poisonous air. At last her hand hit the wood frame of her door.

She moaned in relief as her fingers gripped the brass doorknob. It wasn't hot. Relief gave her strength as she tugged it open and staggered into the hallway, clutching Morris with all her might.

Gillian fell to her knees and began to crawl, recalling some faraway instruction that she was supposed to do this in a fire. In truth, she simply didn't have the strength to stand any longer.

That's when she saw him, standing at the end of the hallway. She opened her mouth to shout to the man, but nothing came out.

She looked down at the teddy bear in her hands, pushing on his furry belly with all her might. Trying to make him squeak loud enough for the man to hear so he could help her.

Instead, Morris smiled up at her and said, "You're too late."

Gillian awoke with a start, gasping for breath. A soft yellow glow emanated from the night-light near her bedroom door. It took her a moment to realize that she was safe in her four-poster bed, not in a smoke-filled hallway.

Sweat drenched her white cotton nightgown. It stuck

to her skin as she rose from the bed, panic still clutching her. She tried to breathe, but couldn't seem to suck in any air.

It's just the nightmare, she told herself. *You're all right*.

A moment later, her chest relaxed and precious air poured into her lungs. She clung to the oak bedpost, gasping for more. That was the worst part of the nightmare—the sense that she was suffocating on smoke and couldn't breathe. She closed her eyes, trying not to think about the fact that her parents had probably experienced that same suffocating panic, that same desperate need to escape.

Only they hadn't made it out of the house alive.

Gillian took a deep, calming breath as her anxiety began to ebb. She didn't understand what was happening to her. The fire that had killed her parents and destroyed her home happened over twelve years ago. Why was she suddenly dreaming about it now? For the last few months she'd been plagued by this same nightmare almost every time she closed her eyes.

She tore off her sodden nightgown, then stood in front of the open bedroom window. She welcomed the cool breeze as it washed over her body. Combing her fingers through her long, damp hair, Gillian knew she wouldn't be sleeping again tonight. That was the worst of it. After one of her nightmares, the adrenaline pumping through her veins made sleep impossible.

She turned toward her bed and looked uneasily at

Morris, the teddy bear that lay propped on a pillow. Half of his tawny brown fur was gone and one black bead eye. He was the only thing she'd had left after the fire.

That and the nightmares that now plagued her.

This one had been particularly creepy. Morris had never talked to her in the dream before.

You're too late. That eerie singsong voice kept echoing in her mind. She didn't know what it meant.

Too late to save her parents? That was true.

Too late to save herself? No, she'd been saved. But she had no memory of their horse trainer, Ian Wiley, rescuing her from the house before it had burned to the ground. She had no memories of the fire at all except for this nightmare that kept plaguing her.

Gillian had been trying to put the past behind her for the last twelve years, concentrating on her art and looking toward the future. Only now the past was haunting her and she couldn't seem to escape it.

Which left her with one choice. After all these years, maybe she finally had to stop running and walk back into the fire.

One

Carter Phillips stood in the foyer of the hotel ballroom, trying to determine the perfect time to make his escape. He didn't feel comfortable at fancy parties like this—hating anything that took him away from his horses.

As a veterinarian, Carter preferred spending his time in a barn rather than a ballroom, but working for Quest Stables made events like this a necessary evil. Even if it was for a good cause.

The black-tie affair would raise money for an organization that provided horse therapy to disabled children and adults. Andrew Preston, stable manager at Quest and heir apparent to the family business, had helped Carter organize several of these horse therapy camps back in Kentucky. Carter had seen for himself what a thrill riding a horse could be for a child who wasn't able to walk or run.

Carter slowly scanned the ballroom, relieved that he didn't see anyone he knew. He wasn't in the mood for small talk. His plane had arrived in San Diego at six o'clock this morning and he was still adjusting to the three-hour time difference.

Quest Stables had six horses running at Del Mar this season and Carter had spent most of his day evaluating them at the racing facility. All six horses seemed to have weathered the long flight from Woodford County without any difficulty.

The hardest part of the trip so far was ignoring all the whispers and curious glances at the Del Mar stables. Everyone in the racing world knew about the scandal brewing around Quest and how its most famous prizewinning horse, Leopold's Legacy, was at the center of the storm.

After winning the Kentucky Derby and a stunning victory at Preakness, Leopold's Legacy had been poised to wow the entire racing world by running for the Triple Crown.

Then disaster struck when it was discovered that the stallion might not be a Thoroughbred. A reconfiguration of the Jockey Association's computer system had led to an accusation that Apollo's Ice wasn't the sire of Leopold's Legacy as recorded in the official records. It had stunned the Prestons and Carter himself, who had been certain there was some kind of mistake.

A certainty that had crumbled over time.

Now people in the racing world were throwing around words like *fraud* and *deception* while everyone at Quest Stables was scrambling to separate the fact from the fiction. It was a scandal that could cost the Preston family their reputation as well as a business worth millions.

A scandal that could ultimately cost Carter his job as head veterinarian at Quest.

He raked a hand through his short hair, bristling at the uncomfortable fit of his tuxedo. It was too tight across the back and shoulders, making him feel as though he was bound up in a straitjacket. Something he might need if this issue wasn't resolved soon.

Hell, he'd overseen the covering of Leopold's Legacy's dam, Courtin' Cristy, by Apollo's Ice, a prize-winning stallion at Angelina Stud Farm. He'd even been present at the foal's birth. But he knew DNA tests didn't lie, and when the results had come back with solid evidence showing that Apollo's Ice *wasn't* the sire of Leopold's Legacy, as recorded in the Stud Book, it had shaken Quest Stables to its very core. The Prestons had pulled Leopold's Legacy from the Belmont Stakes and were now working to solve the mystery.

A buzzing sensation in his pocket pulled Carter's mind away from the scandal that had occupied his every waking thought since the discovery two months ago. He tugged the slim cell phone from his pocket, then suppressed a groan when he saw the name on the Caller ID screen.

"Hello, Noah," Carter said into the phone.

"Hey, big brother, I'm surprised you remember my name," Noah teased. "How long has it been since we last talked? Three or four years?"

He swallowed a sigh, all too aware he'd been neglecting his family lately. He missed them, and hearing his brother's voice deepened the ache of loneliness that had been gnawing at him lately. "I was home over Christmas," Carter reminded him.

"That's right," Noah concurred. "I guess it just seems longer because I was stuck in Chicago all winter with the folks while you were soaking up the sun and all those beautiful Southern belles in Kentucky."

He knew his little brother never lacked for female companionship, even at the tender age if twenty-one. Noah's wit and charm provided him with plenty of friends. He lived to party and Carter missed hearing Noah's funny stories even as he worried that his brother would never take life seriously

"It gets cold in Kentucky, too," Carter told him, moving toward the display cases set up in the center of the ballroom.

The California Horse Breeders Association was holding a silent auction as part of the fund-raiser. Since he and Andrew Preston shared an interest in the charity,

Andrew had asked him to buy something on behalf of the Preston family and make sure the bid was high enough to win. Although the Preston's made generous contributions to several worthy charities, this year Quest Stables needed all the good publicity it could get.

"I'm sure Kentucky is nice and hot in August," Noah replied.

"You're right, but I'm in San Diego at the moment," Carter replied. "We've got horses running at Del Mar."

"So this Leopold's Legacy problem hasn't screwed things up for the other horses at Quest?" Noah asked him.

He should have known his brother would have heard about the scandal. The news about Leopold's Legacy had been splashed across every newspaper in the country with headlines like: Derby Winner a Phony and Triple Crown Contender from the Wrong Side of the Track.

ESPN Magazine had added to the feeding frenzy with an in-depth article about the horse's mystery sire entitled: "Who's Your Daddy?" That was also the question Carter was trying so hard to answer.

Right now, it was only Leopold's Legacy who was not allowed to race, but if they didn't find answers soon, the local and regional racing commissions would enact a ban against all horses majority-owned by Quest.

He grabbed a glass of champagne from a passing waiter as he entered the ballroom and took a deep sip. It wasn't to his taste, since he preferred his liquor hard and strong, just like his women. Not that Carter had found much time for romance since this scandal with Leopold's Legacy had erupted.

"Hey, are you there" Noah asked.

Carter blinked, realizing he'd let his mind wander again. "Yes, I'm still here."

"Well, one of the reasons I'm calling is that you just got a late invitation to your fifteenth high school reunion. It's this weekend."

"Just throw it away," Carter told him.

"You're not coming back for it?"

He heard the disappointment in Noah's voice, but Carter knew he couldn't even consider going home until this mess with Leopold's Legacy was cleared up. The Prestons were like a second family to him and he couldn't abandon them now. "There's no way I can make it. I've got too much work to do."

"That's what you always say," Noah replied. "I think you should try to have some fun for a change and the reunion sounds like a blast."

He checked his watch, realizing he didn't have much time left to bid. "I'm at a charity auction right now and while I wouldn't exactly call it fun, I do need to bid on something." Carter scanned the multitude of items on display. "I'm trying to decide between a set of Limoges china, an authentic silk kimono, and an old saddlebag that was used on the pony express. Which one do you think I should bid on?"

"Can't you just fly to Chicago for the weekend?"

Noah persisted. "I'd like to talk to you about some-thing…."

That's when Carter saw it.

His heart skipped a beat as he stared at a breathtaking portrait of Leopold's Legacy. Or rather a bay horse that looked like Leopold's Legacy's identical twin. The stallion in the painting had the same clover-shaped star on its forehead and the same unique flaxen color in its tail.

But there was something more.

The artist had captured the same spirit that Carter saw in Leopold's Legacy. The majestic stallion in the painting had his head turned toward the sun, the light gleaming off the powerful muscles in his neck and shoulders.

Carter couldn't believe this was just a coincidence. The horse in the painting wasn't Leopold's Legacy, but it looked as if they might have the same bloodline and very possibly the same sire.

"Carter?" Impatience laced Noah's voice. "Are you still there?"

"I'm sorry," he said, barely able to think, much less talk coherently. "I've got to go."

"All right, but call me back. I really need to talk to you."

"Okay," Carter said, barely comprehending his brother's words as he slipped the cell phone back into his pocket. He was too fascinated by the portrait and the possibility it presented.

Carter watched a man wearing a ten-gallon hat make

a bid on the painting. The silent auction was ending soon and he didn't have time to waste.

"Only fifteen minutes left, sir," said a middle-aged woman with a name tag that proclaimed her as Shirley Biden. "So make your bid count."

Carter picked up the pencil and a bidding slip from the table. "What can you tell me about this painting?"

"It's called *Picture of Perfection*," she replied. "That's the name of the horse, too. If you're the top bidder, I've arranged it so you not only win the painting, but get an opportunity to meet the artist."

He stared at the painting, his gut telling him that Picture of Perfection might hold the key to his search for Leopold's Legacy's true sire. At the very least, it could be a first step toward solving the mystery that plagued Quest Stables.

"Ten minutes, sir," Shirley said cheerfully.

Although Carter had been asked to bid on an item for Quest Stables, he'd find something else for them. He scribbled down a figure that would make his accountant drop him as a client, but he wanted this painting for himself.

He signed his name to the bid, then handed it to the woman. Her eyebrows shot up when she looked at the number. "Thank you very much, sir. And good luck."

Carter placed another bid on the vintage leather saddlebag for the Preston family, knowing how much matriarch Jenna Preston liked antiques. Then he paced the ballroom, waiting for the silent auction to end.

He found himself wondering about the identity of Picture of Perfection's dam as well as when and where she had been bred. Artificial insemination was forbidden by the Jockey Association and the International Thoroughbred Racing Federation, which meant Thoroughbreds had to be conceived the old-fashioned way. He and Brent Preston, Andrew's brother and Quest's head breeder, had actually watched the breeding between Apollo's Ice and Courtin' Cristy at Angelina Stud Farm. That's what made the DNA results for Leopold's Legacy so incomprehensible.

Carter declined the offer of a second glass of champagne from a passing waiter, wanting to keep a clear head. He needed information about Picture of Perfection such as breeding date, birth date and genealogical data before he could make any solid determinations. Anything that might point him toward a possible connection with Leopold's Legacy.

Carter found himself standing in front of the portrait, staring at the horse. There was no denying the talent of the artist. The horse looked as if it could leap off the canvas at any moment. He read the artist's signature at the bottom left corner.

G. Cameron.

He wondered if Mr. Cameron had any of the answers he sought. Not likely, but he could probably lead Carter to the owner of the horse.

The chime of bells sounded in the ballroom, signaling the end of the auction. Carter tensed as the director of the charity took the stage. He was a robust man with a full mustache and beard. Carter recognized him as one of the bigwigs at the Del Mar racetrack.

"First, I want to thank each and every one of you for your generous contributions this evening. With your support, we can make a difference in the lives of so many people."

Carter didn't begrudge the money he'd bid on the painting. If he won, at least he knew it was going to a good cause. During college, he'd spent his summers working at a horse camp for disabled kids. That's when he'd developed a love for horses. He'd seen the way they reacted to the children, exhibiting a gentleness that had amazed him.

The director signaled the band for a drumroll, then beamed at the crowd gathered around the stage. "And now it's the time we've all been waiting for—the winners of tonight's auction."

Carter tensed, wondering if he should have placed a higher bid. He had no experience with the art world. Perhaps the painting was worth three times the amount he had bid. Maybe he should have kept Noah on the line and asked his opinion.

His brother had taken a couple of art appreciation classes along with some other courses that Carter had considered pretty worthless for an economics major. Not that Noah ever listened to his advice. However, now Carter saw that there might be some value to them.

"The high bid of the evening is for the lovely horse

portrait by local up-and-coming artist Gillian Cameron of Robards Farm."

Gillian?

For some reason, Carter had just assumed the artist was a man, since the sport of horse racing tended to be dominated by men. That was slowly changing and Quest Stables jockey Melanie Preston was proof of it. She could definitely hold her own with any man on the race-track.

"And the winner is…."

The director paused for dramatic effect and Carter felt as though he might burst out of his skin.

"Dr. Carter Phillips."

The crowd applauded as he released a deep sigh of relief. He'd bid high enough after all and won the painting.

The director moved onto the next item on his list and Carter forced himself to pay attention until he heard that the Prestons had won the vintage saddlebag.

Shirley approached him, her face wreathed with a smile. She reminded him of his favorite aunt back in Chicago.

"Congratulations, Dr. Phillips," she gushed. "I could see how much you liked that portrait."

"Thank you."

She turned toward the painting and clasped her hands together in delight. "Picture of Perfection is such a beautiful horse. I've actually seen him run in some California races this summer. He's very fast and causing quite a sensation around here."

Just like Leopold's Legacy.

Carter shook that thought from his head, not ready to leap to any conclusions. He needed to find the evidence to support his theory.

"Would you like to take the portrait with you now or have it delivered?"

"I'll take it with me," Carter replied. "Can you wrap it up?"

"Certainly. What about the saddlebag?"

Carter thought about it for a moment. "I'd like you to mail that to Jenna Preston at Quest Stables in Woodford County, Kentucky."

"Very good," she said, then leaned toward him and lowered her voice. "I'm so sorry about all the trouble you folks are having. I hope everything works out for the best."

"I appreciate it," Carter said, then broached the subject that really interested him. "I also won the opportunity to meet the artist, right? I'd like to set that up as soon as possible."

Shirley chuckled at his enthusiasm. "Of course. I'll just need your contact information."

Carter took out one of his business cards, then jotted down the name of his hotel and his room number. "My cell phone number is on here, as well, so you can reach me anytime."

"I'll get in touch with the artist and let you know what time works best for her," she replied, taking the card from him.

"The sooner, the better," he said, hoping she'd be free tomorrow. He'd only be in San Diego a couple of weeks and wanted to make every minute count. He loved this area of the country and looked forward to spending a little time outside of the Del Mar racetrack.

As Carter left the ballroom, he wondered if the artist had been at the charity benefit tonight. She might have been able to tell him something about the horse and its lineage.

Then again, she might only want to talk about her art. He admired people with that kind of talent, but had almost nothing in common with them. He was a man of science and the art world was completely foreign to him.

Thanks to Gillian Cameron, he owned a painting of Picture of Perfection. Now all he wanted was the horse's DNA and he'd be happy.

With any luck, she just might be able to help him get it.

Two

When Gillian Cameron opened the door to the main house on Robards Farm, Carter forgot everything he was going to say.

The woman in the doorway was not what he expected. Her mane of chestnut hair reached almost to her waist and her eyes were the deep, rich green of Kentucky bluegrass. Her face captivated him, as well, open and expressive. Her creamy skin seemed to glow from within and looked so soft that he had to stifle the urge to reach out and stroke her cheek. It was a ridiculous reaction and one that he'd never experienced before.

Carter blamed it on fatigue. He'd been unable to

sleep last night, too keyed up by this new lead into
finding Leopold's Legacy's true sire. He'd spent hours
in front of his laptop, studying the DNA test results
of Leopold's Legacy and Apollo's Ice. He'd even
looked up Picture of Perfection's lineage online and
confirmed that he was also reportedly sired by
Apollo's Ice.

Now all he needed was to convince the owner of the
horse to let him take a blood sample so he could
compare the DNA of all the horses involved. He was
fairly certain Picture of Perfection didn't come from
Robards Farm. The only horses he'd seen grazing in a
nearby pasture were an eclectic assortment of quarter
horses, draft horses and even a few miniature horses.

His meeting with the artist was simply meant to be
a starting point in his search for the truth, but now that
he'd seen Gillian he found himself faltering at the gate
and forgetting the real reason he'd come here.

A smile lifted the corners of her generous pink
mouth. "You must be Dr. Phillips."

He gave a stiff nod, trying to gather his scattered
thoughts. He'd pictured her as some middle-aged
hippie woman with immense talent and an eccentric
sense of style.

Gillian looked more like a sexy model for the
designer jeans she wore. The low-slung blue denim
molded the delicious curve of her hips and hugged a
pair of long luscious legs that seemed to go on forever.
The tail ends of her white cotton blouse were tied just

below her perfect breasts and revealed a golden tan on the generous expanse of bare skin that made it all too east to picture her naked.

"Dr. Phillips?" she said, her brow furrowed.

He met her gaze, suddenly aware of the heat of the California sun on the back of his neck. "Please call me Carter."

"It's very nice to meet you, Carter." She reached out to shake his hand.

"So you're the artist," he said, stating the obvious. He noticed a smudge of yellow paint on her hand as she joined him on the front porch.

"That's right." Gillian hitched her thumbs in the front pockets of her jeans, the movement revealing a tantalizing glimpse of her cleavage. "Are you ready?"

"Ready?" he echoed, sounding like an idiot. It might help if he could string more than one or two words together at a time. "Ready for what?"

Amusement danced in her green eyes. "Ready to see Picture of Perfection. That's why you came here today, isn't it?"

"The horse is here?" he asked in surprise, looking around the place. He was no snob, having grown up in a working-class neighborhood in Chicago, but horse racing was an expensive business. Robards Farm looked too run-down to support such an endeavor. There was paint peeling off the house and outbuildings, as well as several pieces of farm machinery that looked as if they were in disrepair.

There were homey touches, as well, like the old tire swing hanging from the oak tree in the center of the yard and the gingham curtains in the window.

"Where else would he be? Gillian asked. "He's in the south pasture."

Carter nodded, aware that he was still adjusting to his surprise that the artist was a beautiful young woman instead of an eccentric. He needed to refocus and concentrate on his purpose for coming here.

"I can't wait to see how close your portrait of Picture of Perfection comes to the real thing," Carter told her.

"Then let's go," Gillian said, stepping off the porch to lead the way.

Carter enjoyed the sexy view from behind for a moment before lengthening his stride to catch up with her. Gillian moved briskly, the sun shining on her hair and turning some of the stray curls bouncing over her shoulders to a deep, burnished copper.

She glanced over at him and smiled, the gleam in her beautiful green eyes giving him the same sensation he used to feel when doing belly flops into the beach on Lake Michigan as a kid.

Femme fatale.

Those were the perfect words to describe Gillian Cameron. Carter had never really known a woman who fit that description the way she did. He hesitated to use the phrase now, although the effect she was having on him left no doubt that he found her desirable.

"We're almost there," Gillian promised.

She stopped to unlatch a white gate that hung crookedly on its hinges. Then she lifted the gate up on one end so it swung open wide enough for them both to pass through it.

Carter waited while she closed the gate and latched it again. He wanted to ask her why Mr. Robards hadn't used some of his prize money from the races Picture of Perfection had won to do some upkeep on the farm. As a veterinarian, he knew faulty gates and fences could lead to animals escaping and getting hit by a car or falling prey to a predator.

"Looks like you could use a handyman to fix that gate," he said.

She sighed. "I'll get to it one of these days. It just seems like there's never enough time to get everything done around here."

An artist and a farmhand. He wondered what other talents she possessed.

They climbed a small knoll, the meadow grass reaching almost to his knees. Then he saw a white gazebo in the distance.

"That's my refuge," Gillian announced.

He followed her there, impressed at the way she'd transformed it into a makeshift artist's studio. There was an easel with a partially completed painting on it, as well as a small table full of bristle brushes and paint.

"It's very nice," he said, noting how the breeze fanned her hair around her face.

Gillian smiled. "It might be a bit unorthodox, but I

do my best work out here. I have the most inspiring view in the world."

He turned to look beyond the gazebo and his breath caught in his throat. Lush green valleys dotted with horses lay between her gazebo and the Pacific Ocean. He recognized the horizon as the same one in the painting he'd just bought. Somehow, she'd been able to embrace the beauty of nature around her and make it come alive on the canvas.

"Come and have a look at my work in progress." Gillian led him farther into the gazebo. "I could use a second opinion."

Carter followed her inside, his eyes going immediately to the easel. "You're doing another painting of Picture of Perfection?"

She sighed. "I can't seem to stop painting him. His name is my curse, because no matter how hard I try I can't seem to achieve perfection."

Carter disagreed. Everything about her was perfect. Her painting, her eyes, her bewitching smile. He moved closer to the easel. "It looks perfect to me. What's wrong with it?"

"I don't know," she said, shaking her head. "It just feels like something is missing. No matter how many times I paint this horse, I'm just not able to move on. I guess I'm looking for something I can't explain."

Carter turned to her. There was a vulnerability about Gillian that touched him, yet she definitely wasn't the damsel-in-distress type. The dichotomy only deepened his curiosity about her.

"How long have you been painting?" he asked.

"About twelve years. I started shortly after I moved here. Herman Robards is my godfather and has never discouraged me from trying new things." She smiled. "Even really stupid things."

"We've all done really stupid things."

She arched a winged brow. "Including you?"

"Sure," he replied. "Some are easy to forget, but others stick with you for much too long. Sometimes forever."

She moved closer to him. "Tell me one stupid thing you've done."

He blinked, surprised by the request. This was supposed to be a simple meeting between an artist and the buyer of her painting. Now it was becoming surprisingly personal.

"Well, let's see...," he began, trying to think of something innocuous.

It had been a very long time since he'd done anything impulsive. Carter had gotten so used to suppressing his own needs and desires to help others that sometimes he felt as if he were just going through the motions of life. It had created an emptiness inside of him that he could usually ignore until someone like Gillian came along. Her vitality and spirit stirred something long dormant inside of him.

"I think you're stalling," she teased.

"I got a tattoo when I was a freshman in college," he blurted.

She wrinkled her brow in confusion. "Why is that stupid?"

He smiled. "Because I'd had too much to drink at the time and did it on a whim. I didn't give any thought to what the tattoo image should be, I just picked one that appealed to me. Then I spent the next two years covering it up with a bandage."

Gillian laughed, a sound so enthralling that he ached to hear again.

"Was it that bad?" she asked.

"The art was okay, I guess. Quite good, actually. It was the image I chose that was stupid."

Curiosity lit her face. "What was it?"

"A butterfly."

Her eyes widened. "I think that's a wonderful choice!"

He laughed. "But not the most masculine one. I was a skinny college kid trying to impress girls. Telling them I had picked a butterfly tattoo because I liked the colors wasn't the best pickup line in the world."

"It would have worked on me," Gillian said softly, then she flushed. "I mean, I'm an artist, so I like colors. May I see it?"

Again, Carter was surprised by the request. Gillian didn't stand on pretense. She was forthright, yet in a way that made him want to accommodate her.

Carter removed his jacket, then rolled up the short sleeve of his shirt to reveal the small butterfly on his bicep.

"Oh, it's gorgeous," she breathed, stepping closer to him. Her slender fingers reached out to trace the intricate design.

His body tightened at her soft touch and he had to remind himself to breathe. Standing this close to Gillian made him realize how very long it had been since he'd held a woman in his arms.

Gillian stepped away from him all too soon. "I think it's a perfectly wonderful tattoo and does not in any way qualify as a stupid mistake. At least you don't cover it with a bandage anymore."

"I've gotten past the embarrassment, for the most part. I'm certainly not a teenager anymore and stopped trying to impress people years ago."

She cocked her head to one side. "So how old are you, Carter?"

"I'm thirty-three."

She grinned. "I'm twenty-two."

Her age his him like a punch in the gut. *Twenty-two.* The eleven-year age difference gaped as wide and deep as the Grand Canyon in his mind. She was barely out of her teens and he'd been fantasizing about her naked….

Carter closed his eyes, realizing that she was almost the same age as Noah, his impulsive and immature little brother. Noah had often scoffed at Carter's stoic predictability and no doubt Gillian would feel the same if she got to know him better. They were both too young to realize that life had a way of interfering with your dreams.

"I'll be twenty-three next month," she proclaimed.

Next month he'd be back in Kentucky. He looked at her, aware that her age had come as a shock to him because Gillian had painted a portrait with such a mature and unique perspective. There was something about her, something he couldn't name. That made her seem wise for her years.

The whinny of a horse drew their attention to the magnificent stallion in the pasture. He stood only a few feet from the gazebo, close enough for Carter to get a good look at him.

"There he is," Gillian said with a note of awe in her voice. "Picture of Perfection. I think his name fits him, don't you?"

Carter's breath hitched. Picture of Perfection really was the spitting image of Leopold's Legacy. "He's a three-year-old?"

She nodded. "He turned three in February. I was there when he was born. I'll never forget that night." She looked up at him. "You're a veterinarian, right? So it's probably pretty routine for you."

"A birth is never routine. It always feels like a miracle to me."

She reached out to grasp his forearm. "Exactly! The only thing I can compare it to is the feeling I get when

I'm painting a horse and everything is going just right. I'm completely focused on what's happening in front of me and tuning everything else out. It's like I'm…."

"Touching the horse's soul?" Carter ventured, then realized how much of himself he'd revealed. That was how he felt whenever he participated in a birth, only he'd never been able to find the right words to describe the experience.

"Yes," she breathed, staring up at him.

Their gazes locked for a long moment, then she looked away, breaking the connection. "I suppose we should head back. Herman's making lunch today and he always worries if I'm late."

He wondered why she lived with her godfather instead of her parents, but unlike Gillian, he wasn't about to ask such a personal question.

"Why don't you come to the house and I can introduce you to him?" Gillian suggested. "He wants to meet the man who bought his favorite painting. In fact, he'll probably invite you to stay for lunch."

The thought of spending more time with Gillian appealed to him. She had a way of making him forget his problems and that was a rare experience for Carter.

As they walked back to the house, Gillian made small talk all the way. She asked him about his work at Quest Stables and how he'd gotten interested in veterinary medicine.

To his surprise, Carter found himself talking about the

injured squirrel he'd nursed back to health when he was ten and the horse camps he'd worked at as a teenager.

Then their conversation turned to Quest Stables and the horses running at Del Mar.

"Do you have any horses entered in the Pacific Classic?" she asked, referring to the annual million-dollar horse race at the Del Mar racetrack. "Picture of Perfection will be racing there."

"Not this year." Carter was surprised that she seemed unaware of the scandal surrounding Leopold's Legacy, who had been scheduled to run in the Pacific Classic, too. The winner of the race earned an automatic berth in the Breeders' Cup Classic.

"Quest Stables has several horses running their maiden race at Del Mar in the week prior to the Pacific Classic," he continued. "We like the competition here and the quality of the track. It's a good place for a horse to start its career."

"Then I look forward to seeing you there," Gillian said. "I want to paint Picture of Perfection at the race-track. So far I've limited myself to pasture portraits, so this will be a whole new challenge for me."

The challenge for Carter would be keeping his mind on his work if Gillian came around. His busy schedule usually didn't leave much time for socializing, especially with a tantalizing femme fatale who was much too young for him.

The door opened when they reached the front porch

and a big bear of a man walked out to meet them. He was the same height as Carter and twice as wide.

"Hello, Herman," Gillian greeted him, confirming for Carter that this was Robards.

Herman grinned at his goddaughter. "Have I got a surprise for you."

Three

Gillian Cameron didn't know if she could take any more surprises today. She was still reeling from finding Carter Phillips at her door. The man was gorgeous, with his short dark hair and eyes as blue as the California sky. Better still, he wasn't one of those insufferable men who knew he was handsome and expected her to fall at his feet.

He was older, too, which was a welcome change from some of those goofballs she'd dated in art school. Even though she'd just met Carter, Gillian liked what she saw. Not only his physical appearance, but the thoughtful way he talked to her and, even better, the way he listened.

She could feel his gaze on her now and it made the back of her neck tingle. He hadn't thought she was a freak when she talked about how painting made her feel. He didn't question why she was twenty-two years old and still living in her godfather's house. He didn't try to make a pass at her, which was a nice change from her usual encounters with men.

Not that this was a *date*. Far from it. Carter was simply the man who had bought her painting. The fact that he seemed so interested in Picture of Perfection was probably one the reasons she was so drawn to him.

Not that she'd mind a date with him. More than one, if she was honest with herself. She was definitely tempted to run her hands over a lot more than his tattoo. The man was the textbook definition of tall, dark and sexy.

"Herman, this is Dr. Carter Phillips," she said, making the introductions. "He bought my painting at the charity fund-raiser last night."

"Nice to meet you," Herman said, reaching out to pump the man's hand.

Unlike most people that Gillian observed, Carter didn't wince at Herman's powerful grip.

"I didn't mean to be rude before," Herman told him. "I was just so darn excited to see Gillian at the door that I couldn't keep it in any longer."

"Excited about what?" Gillian asked, perplexed by his demeanor. Herman looked as if he was about ready to jump out of his snakeskin cowboy boots.

"That gallery owner called," he replied with a twinkle in his brown eyes. "You know, the guy who likes your horse portraits so much."

"Jon Castello?" She'd met the owner of the Arcano Gallery at an art symposium last spring. He'd given a lecture and offered critiques for individual artists. To Gillian's delight, he'd been impressed with her work. She'd been to his gallery a couple of times since then and he'd insisted on becoming her mentor.

"That's the one," Herman replied. "Anyway, he wants you to do a show at his gallery."

Gillian's heart skipped a beat. Her dream had always been to have her art on public display, but she'd never expected it to happen so early in her career.

"Oh, Herman," she said, trying not to get too excited, "are you sure you understood him right? You know how you get phone messages confused sometimes."

"I'm sure," Herman affirmed. "I made him repeat it to me three times just so I wouldn't get the message wrong. I think he was getting a little irritated. No offense, but I think the guy's kind of a jerk."

That didn't surprise her. Like many artists, Jon could be temperamental and had a quick-fire temper. There were times that Gillian wondered if his interest in her was more that professional, but he'd never said or done anything inappropriate.

"I wrote down his number and put it on the desk in your room," Herman continued. "You're supposed to call him as soon as possible to set up a date for the opening of your show."

Her show.

Gillian leaped into Herman's arms, hugging him tightly. He'd always supported her art, even when she'd been plagued with doubts about how long she could keep her dream of an art career alive before she had to give it up to pursue another profession.

Now it seemed her goal of making a living as an artist was coming true even sooner than she'd planned. *If it was a success…*

Gillian shook that thought from her head, still not allowing herself to look too far into the future. She needed to take this rare opportunity one day at a time so she didn't screw things up.

"Why don't you go make that call to Mr. Castello," Herman suggested, "while I offer your young man here a cool drink."

A hot blush crawled up her neck. "He's not my young man," she said quickly, glancing at Carter. "He just came to see Picture of Perfection."

Herman winked at Carter. "Seems to me we've got a picture of perfection standing right in front of us. Don't you agree, Phillips?"

The heat burned her cheeks. "Herman, please."

Her godfather chuckled as he turned to Carter. "It's my goal to make her blush at least once a day. I hear it's good for the complexion."

"I need to go make that phone call," Gillian said,

eager to escape before Herman embarrassed her any
further.

Herman liked to tease her, but he didn't usually do
it in front of strange men. She couldn't help but notice
Carter had avoided answering his question about her
so-called perfection.

Gillian retreated to her bedroom suite, the walls
plastered with her paintings. Most of them were of
horses, although she had tried one of Herman and
Marie a few years ago. It wasn't very good and led to
her decision to stop trying to paint people. She just
couldn't seem to capture them as well as she did
horses.

Gillian found the message Herman had left on her
desk and stared at the name and number scribbled in his
bold, distinct handwriting. It was amazing how this
simple phone call might change her entire life. She'd
learned early that life was a series of sudden twists and
turns, often leading in an unexpected direction.

Like the fire that had killed her parents.

She'd gone to bed that night the beloved daughter
of Mark and Cara Cameron, then found herself
orphaned before dawn the next morning.

It was all so long ago. That's why she didn't understand why she'd been having these nightmares lately.
She hoped her upcoming gallery exhibit would keep
her too busy to worry about the past. Her nightmares
had become so disturbing, she'd even thought about
contacting a hypnotherapist. Yet, she couldn't quite

bring herself to do it. Some part of her was still hoping these nightmares would go away on their own.

As she sat down at her desk and picked up the cordless phone, she wondered what Herman and Carter were talking about. Hopefully, Herman wasn't bragging about her as he had a tendency to do. That might drive Carter right out the door and she wanted the chance to tell him goodbye.

What she really wanted was for him to ask her out on a date.

"First things first," Gillian murmured to herself.

Daydreaming about the sexy hunk downstairs wouldn't get her any closer to her dream of a gallery exhibit. She just had to dial the number and let fate lead her the rest of the way.

Herman led Carter into the sunny kitchen, where the savory aroma of chili filled the air.

"What's your pleasure?" Herman asked him as he opened the refrigerator. "I've got some good Mexican beer or do you prefer something stronger?"

"Beer is fine," Carter replied, glancing around the room. Faded linoleum covered the floors and a small table and chairs stood in the center of the room. He could smell the aroma of cilantro in the air and his mouth watered. Carter liked to cook, but didn't find much time to do it during racing season.

Herman pulled two frosty bottles of beer out of the refrigerator and handed one of them to Carter. Then he took a seat at the table. "Pull up a chair and make yourself comfortable. Gillian will be a while. That Castello guy never stops talking."

It occurred to Carter that he didn't need to stay until Gillian returned. He just needed to get Herman's permission to take a blood sample from Picture of Perfection and he could be on his way.

On the other hand, he wasn't in a hurry. He had looked over the Quest horses this morning and would do so again tonight. They all seemed to be in good shape and ready to be put through their paces tomorrow.

Carter sat down and took a long sip of his beer, savoring the way it washed down the back of his throat.

"Hope you don't mind waiting for her in the kitchen," Herman said. "This is where I spend most of my time. My Marie always wanted me to entertain guests in the parlor, but that's much too fussy for an old cowboy like me. Now that she's gone, I just bring folks here. Seems more homey, don't you think?"

Carter agreed, hoping the informal atmosphere would make the man agreeable to his request. He took another sip of his beer, wondering how best to broach the subject of a blood test.

"You're a veterinarian, aren't you?" Herman asked him. "I think that's what Gillian told me."

"That's right. I work for Quest Stables in Woodford County, Kentucky."

Herman nodded. "They raise some mighty fine horses there. Do you suppose they'd mind my asking you for a second opinion? I'm sure they only hire the best. I'm willing to pay of course."

Carter leaned forward, sensing an opening. "I'm always happy to offer advice. Is this about a horse?"

Herman shook his head. "No, my dog, Ranger. He's a border collie and he's come up kinda lame these last few weeks. My old vet retired to Florida last Christmas. I'm just not sure this new vet we hired knows what's really wrong with him."

"What's he told you?

"That it's probably a muscle strain and it just needs time to heal. The only thing is that Ranger doesn't seem to be getting any better."

"I can look at him now, if you want."

Herman chuckled. "Well, the thing is, he's not so bad that he can't wander off. I haven't seen Ranger in a while. He's probably out chasing rabbits, though he certainly can't run fast enough to catch them."

Carter could see that Herman cared about his dog, just as the Prestons cared about all the horses at Quest. His respect for the man was growing by the minute.

"Did your vet do any lab work on him?" Carter asked him. Maybe instead of taking money for his opinion, Herman would agree to let him have a vial of Picture of Perfection's blood. A barter that would satisfy both of them.

"Nope. I'll show you what I've got." Herman slid off his stool and disappeared from the kitchen. He returned a few minutes later with a thin file folder in his hand.

"Here's Ranger's health records from the day he was born."

Carter took the file from him and scanned the pages inside.

"It all looks fairly normal."

"That's good I suppose." He tipped his beer bottle up and drained it. With a satisfied sigh, he set the empty bottle on the table. "Are you ready for another round?"

"Not quite yet." Carter wasn't certain he could keep up with the man. He watched Herman retrieve another beer from the refrigerator, then waited until he sat back down to broach the subject that had brought him here today.

"I'm hoping you might be able to do a favor for me."

Herman reached for the bottle opener. "Name it."

"I assume you've heard about the problem with Leopold's Legacy?"

Herman nodded. "A real shame. That horse had Triple Crown winner written all over him. Any idea what happened there?"

Carter shook his head. "We're still trying to figure it out. Despite all the rumors, there was no fraud involved. Somehow, Leopold's Legacy was sired by another stallion. We just don't know which one or how it happened. If we don't figure it out soon, all the other horses majority-owned by Quest will be banned from racing."

Herman furrowed his brow. "And you think I can help in some way?"

Carter sucked in a deep breath. "I knew you could help as soon as I saw that portrait of Picture of Perfection at the silent auction. He looks like the identical twin of Leopold's Legacy."

Herman was silent and Carter gave him time to soak in the information.

"I think it's very possible," Carter said at last, "that the same stallion that sired Picture of Perfection was also the sire for Leopold's Legacy. But the only way I can prove it is with a blood test."

"You don't need a blood test. I can tell you that Picture of Perfection was sired by Apollo's Ice."

"We thought the same thing about Leopold's Legacy."

Herman got up from his stool and walked over to the large kitchen window that overlooked the rolling meadow. He stood there a while, not saying anything, and Carter wondered what he was thinking about.

At last, Herman turned around, an odd expression on his face. "So let me get this straight," he said slowly. "You want me to give you permission to do a blood test to prove that Picture of Perfection *wasn't* sired by Apollo's Ice? Even when all his records say otherwise?"

"Quest Stables found out the hard way that the records for Leopold's Legacy were wrong. The same thing could happen to Picture of Perfection."

"That would be a strange coincidence, don't you think?"

"I'd think you'd want to know the truth, one way or the other."

Herman met his gaze. "It's a hell of a lot for someone to ask."

"I know." He didn't have a clue what Herman was thinking, but Carter knew he couldn't back down now. Not when he was this close. "Will you let me do it?"

Gillian suddenly appeared in the open kitchen doorway, her green eyes blazing with anger. "Over my dead body."

Four

Gillian hadn't meant to eavesdrop, but Carter's words had frozen her in the doorway, their impact hitting her like a fist. He hadn't purchased her portrait of Picture of Perfection because he liked her art. He hadn't spent time with her because he was interested in her as an artist or as a woman.

It had all been a ruse.

Carter turned around to face her. "Gillian...I didn't see you..."

She held up one hand, refusing to let him fool her again. "It's time for you to leave."

Herman's eyes widened at her tone, but he sat back in his chair without saying a word.

Carter cleared his throat. "I don't know what you heard, but…"

"I heard the real reason you're here," she interjected. "And the answer is no, so there's nothing left for you to say."

Carter glanced at Herman, then back at Gillian. "If you'll just let me explain…"

"Explain what?" she cried. "That you want to try and prove that Picture of Perfection isn't a Thoroughbred? That the reputation of Quest Stables is more important to you than your own integrity?"

His blue eyes hardened. "You're wrong about me. I'm not out to hurt either one of you, but the truth has a way of coming out."

"Is that supposed to be some kind of threat?" she asked incredulously.

"Take it as a friendly warning."

Something twisted inside of her. She hated the fact that her instincts had let her down. Again. Carter had fooled her completely. What he wanted could only hurt her, and Gillian wasn't about to let that happen.

"Picture of Perfection looks identical to Leopold's Legacy," he explained. "It's only logical to suspect that they might share the same sire. I'm not trying to pull a fast one on you."

"Really?" she exclaimed, wondering how he could keep a straight face. "You've been deceiving me since I met you. Pretending to be interested in that portrait and in my art."

And in me, she added silently to herself.

"I am interested," he insisted.

Gillian couldn't listen to him anymore. She walked out of the kitchen and headed for the front door, disappointment welling inside of her. All she wanted to do was escape to the sanctuary of her bedroom and forget she'd ever met him.

"Gillian, wait," he implored. "I don't want to leave like this. Why don't you and I and Herman sit down and talk this out."

She turned around, steeling herself against a change in his tactics. "There's something you should know before you leave. My ranch borders Herman's land, I use his pasture, but Picture of Perfection belongs to me. I'm the only one who can give you what you want."

Carter stared at her. "All I want is one small vial of blood."

"The answer is no."

He hesitated for a moment, as if he wanted to say something else, then he walked out the door.

Gillian slammed it behind him, wishing she'd never set eyes on Carter Phillips.

"He sure got you all riled up."

She turned to see Herman standing in the foyer, a bemused smile on his face.

"I can't remember the last time I saw you lose your temper like that," he said, rubbing his hand across his gray whiskers. "Seems like it might be about more than the horse."

She took a deep breath. Maybe she had overreacted just a bit. In truth, the constant nightmares and the lack of sleep had left her with a hair-trigger temper. Her emotions had been so raw lately that Carter's deception had caught her completely off guard.

As her anger ebbed away, a deep sadness filled the void. "I'm just tired of men who can't be trusted."

His smile faded as walked over to her and looped one arm around her shoulder. "I'm sorry, Gilly."

"You know I don't mean you, Herman." She leaned into his shoulder, grateful for the comfort he always provided her. Her godfather might have let her down in the past, but she'd never doubted his love for her.

He kissed the top of her head. "Forget about Dr. Phillips. The way you laid into him, I don't think he'll be back here again."

She forced a smile. "I hope you're right."

"I'm always right," he said with a chuckle, then he headed for the door. "Maybe I should make sure he doesn't take a detour around the pasture on his way out. The man doesn't strike me as the sneaky type, but then you never know."

Gillian watched him leave, then headed to her room. Once inside, she grabbed her sketch pad, seeking the solace that drawing gave her.

The charcoal pencil flew over the paper, the lines coming together to form Carter's square jaw and strong mouth. She worked intensely, never stopping as his face gradually appeared on the paper in front of her.

Shortly after the fire, Gillian's psychologist had suggested art therapy as a way of working through her grief and providing an outlet for her emotions. Gillian had been so full of rage and sadness and confusion and hadn't known how to deal with any of it.

The art therapist had told her to literally draw out her feelings on paper, then dispose of them in some way that would symbolically represent discarding the negative emotions inside of her.

She was certainly ready to dispose of Carter Phillips. As she sat cross-legged on her bed, the sketch pad in her lap, she remembered the way his eyes crinkled when he smiled. The curl of his lashes. The tiny bump in his nose.

As an artist she often noticed little details around her that other people missed. The shape of his ears. The thin scar just above his left eyebrow. The tiny nick in his chin.

Her pencil slowed as she worked on the wave in his dark hair and tried to perfect the set of his blue eyes. When she finally looked up at the clock, she was surprised to find that two hours had passed since she'd begun drawing.

She sucked in a deep breath, realizing that the last time she'd been this absorbed in a sketch was shortly after the fire. That sketch had been of her parents and it had hung in a frame above her dresser for the last twelve years.

Her sketches and paintings had proven more

powerful than any antidepressant in releasing the chains of grief that had bound her soul after the fire. They had also revealed a latent art talent that had flourished under the skilled tutelage of her art therapist.

At last, Gillian put the charcoal pencil down and straightened her legs, wincing at the ache in her stiff knees. She'd been sitting in one place for too long and now her right foot was asleep. She paced the floor, trying to get rid of the pins and needles sensation flooding her foot.

Then she turned back to the bed and stared at the sketch of Carter Phillips. He stared back at her, looking so honest and handsome that she wanted to cry.

Her anger had faded and the desire to crumple up the sketch of Carter and toss him into the trash no longer burned inside of her.

She closed the sketch pad, then set it on her desk. After so many years of therapy, she knew her overreaction to his motives for buying the portrait was a symptom of a deeper problem. The nightmares were starting to take a toll on every aspect of her life. She couldn't prepare for a gallery showing with the lack of sleep she was experiencing. That wouldn't be fair to her or to Jon.

She'd tried sleeping pills in the past, hoping they'd prevent the nightmares or, at the very least, stop the debilitating aftereffects. But the pills only seemed to make things worse. The tranquilizing effect had made it harder for her to waken from the nightmare and left her shaky and dizzy.

Gillian opened the center drawer of the desk and pulled out a slip of paper with a phone number on it. Her best friend had given her the name of a respected hypnotherapist over a week ago, but she'd been putting off making the call.

She stared at the telephone on her desk, wondering if she'd be strong enough to let someone take her back into the past. The nightmares were already painful, but this time she'd be volunteering to relive the heat of the fire, the smoke-filled air, and the panic-stricken terror that had engulfed her that horrible night.

Taking a deep breath, Gillian picked up the receiver and dialed the number.

Five

The earthy scents of horses and hay greeted Carter the next morning as he walked into the stables at the Del Mar racetrack. He'd spent a restless night in his king-size bed at the hotel, Gillian's angry words echoing in his head. He'd risen before dawn to make the twenty-mile trek from San Diego to the seaside city of Del Mar.

As the sun broke over the horizon, it cast a golden glow on the long rows of stables located at the north end of the track. The premier racing facility had stalls for a thousand horses and even at this early hour the place was already bustling with grooms, trainers, jockeys and other racing personnel.

This would be home for the next two weeks as Quest

Stables had six horses running their maiden races. This week the Quest trainers would put the horses through their paces, then they'd begin racing next week. Carter's trip to California would culminate with watching the big race, the Pacific Classic, that had everyone talking.

A shadow of irritation dimmed the bright morning for him as he headed toward the stalls designated for the Quest Stables horses. Before the scandal broke, Leopold's Legacy had been slated to run in this high-stakes race and Carter knew the horse would have been the odds-on favorite to win.

But those odds didn't matter anymore. Leopold's Legacy had been banned from racing, and if they didn't resolve this scandal very soon, the local and regional racing commissions all across North America could decide to ban all the other horses majority-owned by Quest from racing.

Carter couldn't let that happen. His job, and his reputation, depended on it. He had too many people counting on him that he didn't want to disappoint. If only Gillian had listened to reason…

He shook that thought from his head as he reached the first stall. It wasn't Gillian's fault that he'd approached the situation all wrong. He should have been honest about his intentions from the beginning. Of course, then he might have missed that walk out to the gazebo. Missed spending time with the most fascinating woman he'd met in too long to remember.

He bit back a sigh, tired of feeling sorry for himself. He'd learned a long time ago that regret was a useless emotion. It was better to move forward and resist the temptation of pondering what might have been.

He needed to forget about Gillian Cameron. Forget the sound of her laughter the way her green eyes sparkled in the sunlight. The way her body curved in just the right places and how her long, chestnut hair looked softer than silk.

"Yeah," Carter muttered to himself. "Just forget about her. Easiest thing in the world."

"Hey, Phillips, are you talking to yourself again?"

Carter looked up to see Troy Daley, a fellow veterinarian, approaching him. They'd shared more than a few beers and horse stories on the racing circuit. Carter respected his skills as an equine specialist and they often consulted each other on difficult cases.

"Isn't it a little early for you to be up and about?" Carter asked, reaching out to shake his hand.

"One of my horses is running his first race after battling a bowed tendon for the last six months. I need to keep a close eye on him and make sure he's ready to go tomorrow."

Carter nodded, knowing the best treatment for inflammation of the flexor tendon was a long period of rest. He also knew that less than half of the horses who suffered from a bowed tendon came back successfully, which was a testament to Troy's skills.

Troy cleared his throat. "I want to say how sorry I

am that Quest Stables has been caught up in this scandal with Leopold's Legacy. It must be pretty rough on you."

Carter gave a brisk nod. "*Rough* is one word for it. *Frustrating* is another. I was there when the mare, Courtin' Cristy, was bred to Apollo's Ice. Hell, I was there for the birth of Leopold's Legacy. I'm still trying to figure out what happened."

Troy leaned against a wooden post. "So no luck there yet?"

Carter shook his head. "I thought I had a lead, but…it didn't pan out."

He was reluctant to tell Troy about Gillian and her determination to keep Picture of Perfection from having a DNA test. Rumors spread faster than wildfire on the racing circuit. Even an innocent comment by Troy could lead to someone questioning Picture of Perfection's lineage and qualifications to run in the Pacific Classic.

"Well, I hope it all works out for you," Troy said. "If it was me…" He shook his head. "Well, if it was me, I might be tempted to take that teaching position I was offered last month."

Carter looked up. "A professorship? Where?"

"At Texas A&M University. They're looking for an equine specialist. Hell, we could get a job practically anywhere, given our experience on the circuit."

"How much do they pay?"

Troy cocked his head as he looked at Carter. "Why? You interested?"

He hesitated, then shook his head. He had too many responsibilities to even think of pursuing that dream. "I've got my hands full at the moment."

Troy grinned. "I had my hands full last night with a cute redhead I met on the beach. That's what I love best about Del Mar—the beach and the babes in bikinis. It truly is Where The Turf Meets The Surf."

That was the racetrack's slogan and half the betting crowd usually wore beach attire to the races. He wasn't surprised that Troy had already hooked up with one of the locals. The Texas vet was famous for his road trip relationships. Carter had never been tempted to indulge in temporary trysts—until he'd met Gillian Cameron.

Troy pushed himself away from the wooden post. "I'd better get back to work. Maybe we can grab a beer some night soon and I can tell you all about my adventures with the redhead."

"Sounds good," Carter replied, then he turned around and continued his trek down the center aisle of the long stable.

The whispers and sneers had died down, but Carter still found it difficult not to rise to the defense of Quest Stables whenever he heard someone make a snide comment. With the foul mood he was in today, Carter was itching for an excuse to punch someone.

When he reached the Quest stalls, he was relieved to see that all the horses were eating. It was a sign of a healthy animal, though many horses often went off their feed for a day or two after making a cross-country trip.

Quest Stables transported them in a custom-equipped airplane. A few highly strung horses were given sedatives, but Carter liked to avoid that whenever possible.

As he surveyed the six horses, he couldn't see any lingering effects from the flight. He credited the fresh sea air and the beautiful weather. The fact that Del Mar was situated right on the coastline made it one of his favorite venues.

Another reason he liked this track so well was the Polytrack all-weather surface that had been installed a few years ago. The nine-million-dollar racetrack had a high shock absorption rate that decreased the risk of injury to the horses.

As he entered the first stall, Carter silently announced his presence to the two-year-old Thoroughbred by placing one hand on its flank. A spirited filly, Sir Lancelot's Lady acknowledged his arrival by lifting her head in the air and shifting slightly in the stall. He waited until she settled down, then ran his hand down one leg from shoulder to fetlock to check for any areas of swelling.

The horse snorted, rearing back in the stall.

"Easy, there," Carter said gently. He moved to the front of the horse, stroking one hand down her long neck as he made a visual inspection of the filly's eyes and nostrils.

"Looks like Sir Lancelot's Lady is feeling a bit frisky today," said a familiar voice behind him.

He turned around to see Melanie Preston standing in the aisle. She had shirt blond hair and a winning smile. At just five feet tall, she was the shortest of Thomas and Jenna Preston's four adult children and the only girl.

Melanie nodded toward the horse in the next stall. "Do you think Sasquatch will be ready to race tomorrow?"

"He'll be ready if you are," Carter replied.

She grinned, a mischievous twinkle in her light blue eyes. "I'm always ready."

Melanie's slight build and short stature made her chosen career as a jockey the perfect fit for her. She was thirty-one years old and worked hard to stay in top physical condition.

"Any word from Kentucky?" Carter asked, hoping for some good news for a change.

She nodded. "I talked to my father yesterday. He's worried Uncle David's horses are going to outperform Quest this year given the situation with Leopold's Legacy. Personally, I think that's the least of our concerns."

Carter agreed, although he knew about the competitive rivalry between Thomas Preston and his younger brother. After David Preston had moved to Australia and started Lochlain Racing, that rivalry had seemed to intensify. But Thomas's recent visit to Australia, followed by his nephew Shane's trip to Kentucky, had done much to smooth the rough edges in the relationship between the American and Australian Prestons.

"Quest Stables will get through this," Carter assured her. "We've just got to stay tough."

She nodded. "I know how to be tough. I grew up with three brothers, remember?"

Carter looked around the stable. "Speaking of brothers, where is Robbie?"

Robbie Preston was Melanie's younger brother and one of the Quest trainers. He usually arrived at the stables before anyone else in the morning, still trying to prove himself to the family. Carter knew the recent appointment of Marcus Vasquez as head trainer of Quest Stables had left the twenty-eight-year-old Preston with a big chip on his shoulder. Robbie had expected to get the job after the departure of former head trainer Daniel Whittleson, but his parents hadn't thought he was ready for that kind of responsibility.

Carter felt bad for him. Both Robbie and Marcus were excellent horse trainers and the power struggle had caused more than one conflict between them. The tension caused by the scandal didn't help matters, either. That's why it was so critical to Carter to find out the truth.

If only he could convince Gillian to let him do that test. But Carter knew the chances of that happening were now slim to none. She'd have to trust him first, and at this point, it was doubtful she'd ever talk to him again.

"Earth to Carter," Melanie said, looking intently at him. "What?"

"I was telling you that I haven't seen Robbie yet today, but he's obviously not the only one missing in action. Your body might be here, but your mind is definitely somewhere else."

He hesitated, wondering how much he should tell her. Then he realized Melanie had as much at stake as he did. "I found another horse that looks exactly like Leopold's Legacy."

She arched a brow. "And?"

"And I mean *exactly*. He's a bay horse with the same flaxen color in his tail and a clover shaped star on his forehead."

"That seems unusual." A spark of interest lit her eyes. "Where did you find this horse?"

"I bought a painting of him at the charity auction two nights ago. The artist—she's also his owner—is a woman named Gillian Cameron and she's amazing."

"Get to the horse," Melanie said.

"I saw the horse yesterday and found out he was sired by Apollo's Ice."

Melanie took a step toward him. "Are you serious?"

He nodded. "So naturally I asked if I could take a blood sample for a DNA test."

"And?"

"And she turned me down flat. Kicked me out of the house, actually." He paused, remembering the expression of disappointment on Gillian's beautiful face. "I think I may have handled it badly."

"Who cares?" Melanie exclaimed. "We'll find another way to get the blood sample. If he wasn't sired by Apollo's Ice…"

"Then they probably share the same sire and we might be one step closer to finding out the name of that sire and putting Leopold's Legacy back in action."

"One step closer to finally putting this mess behind us," Melanie muttered, then she looked up at him. "What's the name of the horse?"

"The horse is Picture of Perfection and…"

"Picture of Perfection," she said in dismay. "No wonder she kicked you out of the house! He's just the newest rising star on the racing circuit. He's won some important California races this year and is a favorite in the Pacific Classic."

So Shirley Biden hadn't exaggerated in her reports of the horse. Carter had been too caught up with looking for the sire of Leopold's Legacy to stay on top of all the latest racing news. He understood why Gillian had been so adamant about refusing the blood test for Picture of Perfection. She had a lot at stake, too.

"So what's the plan?" Melanie asked him.

"There is no plan. It's over. Gillian Cameron never wants to see me again."

"We could go to the track officials," Melanie suggested, "tell them there might be an issue with Picture of Perfection's lineage…" Her voice trailed off as she shook her head. "No, that's a terrible idea. I can't even believe I considered it."

"I considered it, too," Carter confessed, "for about two seconds. I guess that just shows how desperate we are to find the truth."

Melanie nodded. "Should we tell Robbie and Marcus about this?"

Carter shook his head. "No. At least, not yet. The fewer people that know, the better. Maybe I can approach her again."

That thought had been floating in his mind all morning. He knew it was a long shot, but the more he pondered it, the more he wanted to take the chance. If nothing else, he'd get the opportunity to see Gillian again. Then maybe he could figure out why she seemed to have such a disconcerting effect on his equilibrium.

"I think you should try," Melanie encouraged him, pulling Carter out of the stall. "In fact, go over there right now. Maybe she's had some time to think about the test and changed her mind."

Carter sincerely doubted it. "I haven't finished checking the other horses yet."

"This is more important," Melanie insisted. "We'll only take Sir Lancelot's Lady out until you get back."

Carter started down the aisle, then came to an abrupt halt as he stared at the entrance to the stable.

Melanie came up behind him. "Is something wrong?"

It was a question he didn't know how to answer. He felt a little dizzy and his heart was racing, but he had a perfectly valid explanation for his condition.

Gillian Cameron was walking through the stable door and headed straight for him.

Six

Gillian didn't know what to make of the expression on Carter's face or of the cute little blonde standing close to him.

A little too close in Gillian's opinion.

She kept her gaze on Carter, wondering if he was happy to see her or irritated that she was intruding on his domain. A nervous tingle fluttered in her stomach, but she kept putting one foot in front of the other, intent on going the distance.

For once, her nightmare hadn't tormented her last night. Instead, she'd lain awake in her bed rehearsing this very scene in her head. What she'd say to him, then what Carter would say to her.

In her mind, Gillian always had some snappy retort for any comment he might make, but in the light of day, just the sight of the man made her mouth feel dry and all her prepared words melt away.

When she reached him, Gillian came to a stiff halt, wondering if she looked as foolish as she felt. Despite her trepidation, she tilted up her chin and met his gaze. The worst he could do was refuse her. She'd experienced worse and survived.

"What are you doing here?" he asked.

The blonde next to him folded her arms across her chest and didn't bother to hide her curious stare. Gillian ignored her.

"We need to talk."

"I'm listening."

Gillian looked around the stable and realized other people seemed to be listening, too. It would be hard enough to ask Carter for a favor without an audience looking on.

She licked her dry lips. "Is there somewhere we can go? Somewhere more…private?"

Carter hesitated, then gave a brisk nod. "All right." He turned to the woman beside him. "I'll be back soon, Melanie."

Melanie smiled. "Take your time."

Gillian turned around and started walking toward the stable entrance, not even looking to see if Carter was following her. A hot blush burned in her cheeks as she made her way outside. If she didn't have so much at stake, she'd just keep walking all the way back to her car, Instead, she turned around to find Carter right on her heels.

His nearness startled her and she moved backward a step, almost falling over a plastic bucket. Carter reached out to catch her at the same time she grasped the front of his blue chambray shirt with her hands.

"Are you all right?" he asked.

"Yes," she said, trying to regain her balance. Gillian was all too aware of his strong hands on her arms and the hard muscles of his torso bunching beneath her clenched fingers.

She released her tight grip on his shirt, then tried to smooth the wrinkled fabric by rubbing her hands over his chest. "Sorry about that. I guess I need to watch where I'm going."

He dropped his hands from her and took a step back, a strange expression on his face. Then he leaned down to pick up the bucket and move it out of the way. When he stood back up, the look she'd seen was gone.

She brushed a stray hair off her forehead. "I suppose you're surprised to see me here this morning."

He hesitated a moment. "To tell you the truth, Gillian, I'm glad you're here. I was planning to drive out to your ranch today and apologize."

"Oh?"

A trainer led a horse toward the stable, forcing Gillian and Carter to move off the path. Then Carter motioned toward the tan stucco grandstand. "Let's go to the Patio. No one will interrupt us there."

She followed him past the grandstand to the elevated Seabiscuit Skyroom Patio that offered a panoramic view of the racetrack and the Pacific Ocean. Despite the beautiful vista, Gillian had to admit to herself she had a hard time taking her eyes off Carter.

He was the kind of man who commanded attention and Gillian admired that about him. It was one of the reasons she'd been so hurt when he'd used that charisma to deceive her.

There was no one else on the Patio, giving them the privacy that Gillian craved. She took a deep breath to explain why she'd come here today, but Carter spoke before she could get a word out.

"Like I said before, I owe you an apology." He moved a step closer to her, the warm breeze ruffling his dark hair. "My behavior yesterday was inexcusable. I don't blame you for being angry."

She walked over to the railing, watching the horses run through their paces on the track below. Carter joined her there, his proximity making it difficult for her to think clearly. This was a delicate situation, but Gillian had never been one for subterfuge.

"I need my painting back."

He blinked. "What?"

"The portrait of Picture of Perfection that you bought at the auction. I need it back."

He rubbed a hand over his square jaw. "I know

what painting you're talking about, Gillian, but I'm not going to just give it back to you. I realize you're probably still angry with me, but I paid a lot of money for that painting and…"

"No," she interjected, "that's not it at all."

Despite Gillian's extensive rehearsal, she was handling this all wrong. "You can keep the painting, I just want to borrow it for my opening at the Arcano Gallery. The owner absolutely insists it be shown as part of the full collection."

"Oh." Relief smoothed his face. "Well, that's different."

She smiled. "Good. I don't know how long you're planning to stay in California, but I can ship the portrait back to wherever you live."

"I live in Kentucky and I haven't agreed to let you borrow my painting yet."

She noticed the emphasis he put on the words *my painting* and bristled a little. While Gillian had sold her horse portraits before, this one was her best work and she considered it *her* painting. Still, it wouldn't do any good to quibble with the man, especially since he was proving to be more stubborn than she had imagined.

"I suppose you're waiting for my apology," she said softly. "And I do owe you one, Carter. I'm not sure what came over me yesterday, but I rarely lose my temper like that."

"I'm not looking for an apology," he countered. "I want something else from you."

She stared at him, apprehension prickling her skin. "What?"

"A chance for us to start over."

Gillian wasn't sure she understood him. "We've already apologized to each other and it seems we're now capable of having a civil conversation. What else do you want?"

"I want you to be my date for the Turf Club Ball this Saturday night."

That was only three days away. Gillian had never been to a ball, but she didn't entirely trust Carter's motives. "I should warn you that I'm not going to change my mind about a DNA test for Picture of Perfection."

"That's in the past," he insisted. "We're starting over, remember?"

Gillian wished she could believe him, but she'd been let down by people too many times to count. "I know a lot about starting over. I've had to do it again and again in my life."

She smoothed one hand along the railing, remembering Herman's insistence that she tell him everything so he'd finally understand that a DNA test for Picture of Perfection was out of the question.

"You can trust me, Gillian."

She couldn't help but smile at his words. "I'm afraid that's not going to happen, either. Nothing personal, Carter, but I simply can't afford it. Picture of Perfection is my last hope, the last chance I have to save everything that's important to me."

He frowned. "I don't understand."

"Then let me explain it to you." Her hands curled around the railing as she fought back the emotions that threatened to overtake her. She needed to stay calm and focused. Most of all, she needed to make it perfectly clear that no amount of sweet talk or wooing would make her change her mind about the test. She refused to let Carter or anyone else use her that way.

"Twelve years ago I lost my parents and my home in a fire. I moved in with my godparents, Herman and Marie, who lived on the neighboring ranch."

His expression softened. "You were only ten years old?"

She nodded, her throat tight. "It was a tough time for me. Very tough. With the help of Herman and Marie, I got through it. Herman was the trustee of my estate and he cared for my land and my racehorses just like he did his own. Then, when I was sixteen, another tragedy occurred."

She sensed Carter moving closer to her, but Gillian couldn't let herself look at him until she got through the story. "Marie died of cancer and it felt like losing my mother all over again. It hit Herman even worse. He started spending a lot of time away from the ranch. He never told me where he went and I learned to stop asking."

A cloud floated in front of the sun, casting a shadow over them. "About a year later," she continued, "when I was seventeen, Herman finally told me everything.

He'd been going to the casinos almost every day since Marie's death."

"So he has a gambling addiction?" Carter ventured.

She nodded. "He'd gambled away all of his race-horses as well as mine. His ranch was mortgaged to the hilt, but he'd managed to stop himself and face his problems before he was reduced to selling my land. Since I was a minor, he had full control of my property. I might have lost everything. I still might."

Carter rubbed a hand over his jaw. "How could he do that to you? You'd already lost so much."

Gillian understood his reaction. She'd been just as horrified at the time, but had soon learned enough about addiction to understand that it was a serious illness.

"Herman told me the gambling seemed to numb his pain for a while," she said, "almost like some kind of drug. He'd never been good at expressing his emotions, so Marie's death had left him reeling. Gambling was the only escape he could find."

"It sounds like you've forgiven him."

Gillian finally met his gaze. "Like I said before, I've had a lot of practice at starting over. Herman began at-tending Gambler's Anonymous as well as seeing a private therapist, but we were pretty broke and all our Thoroughbreds were gone. Since we couldn't afford to buy any new animals, I decided to turn my land into a sanctuary for abandoned horses."

His sympathy turned to admiration. "That's pretty impressive."

"It's not a big sanctuary," she said humbly, "just as many horses as can fit in the stables. Even though the main house burned down, all the outbuildings are still there, along with a small cottage where Picture of Perfection's trainer lives."

"Big or small, it's still a hell of a lot more than other people do."

"I just wish it was enough. There are so many abused and neglected horses. I want to find a loving home for each one."

Curiosity crinkled his brow. "You said that Herman sold off all your racehorses to pay for his gambling debts. So how did you come to own Picture of Perfection? Is he one of your abandoned horses?"

She smiled. "No, although that would make a great story. The truth is just as wonderful to me. An elderly woman in Kentucky read a newspaper story about my horse sanctuary and used to send me donations every month to help pay for feed and other necessities. When she died, she left me a pregnant Thoroughbred mare in her will."

He whistled low. "That's a valuable gift."

"More valuable than I ever imagined. Picture of Perfection was born a few months after the mare was transported here. About a year after his birth, we had to sell the mare to pay some outstanding bills, but we kept the colt."

Now it was Carter who couldn't seem to look at her. He stared out at the track, the sun glinting off his dark hair.

"Picture of Perfection is my last chance to save Robards Farm from foreclosure," she said softly. "My last chance to keep the sanctuary afloat. His arrival was a miracle and about the only thing that seems to have gone right in my life. I refuse to lose him...to lose my dream...after I've already lost so much else."

Carter turned to look at her, his voice husky. "Why are you telling me all of this?"

She took a deep breath. "I'm telling you this to keep you from wasting your time. A DNA test for Picture of Perfection is never going to happen. I like you, Carter, but I simply can't risk it. So you may want to invite another woman to the Turf Club Ball."

"I don't want another woman," he said without hesitation.

Gillian's heart contracted at his words, even though she knew he was only talking about a dance. The intensity in his gaze was unnerving and she had to remind herself that any relationship they might form would probably only last as long as Carter was in California.

"Then I accept your invitation," she said evenly.

He smiled. "And I'll be happy to loan you my portrait of Picture of Perfection. When is your gallery exhibit?"

"It opens a week from Friday," she replied, trying not to sound apprehensive about it. "Another artist canceled on Jon, so this truly is my big break. I'll let you know when you can bring the portrait to the gallery."

He nodded. "Perfect. I'm anxious to see your other work."

She laughed. "Some of it will look familiar since Picture of Perfection has been my model for the last several months. I can't seem to let him go."

Gillian wondered if that sounded as strange as it made her feel. She'd never had this kind of obsession with a subject before. It worried her a little and she found herself analyzing her response to see if it meant something more. No matter how many portraits she painted of Picture of Perfection, she couldn't seem to stop, driven to keep painting him until she got it just right.

That kind of perfectionism could be deadly for an artist's creativity, but no other subject inspired her. She hoped her gallery exhibit would provide the impetus she needed to move on.

"So what time can I pick you up for the ball?" Carter asked her. "It starts at eight o'clock on Saturday night."

"How about seven-thirty?"

"Sounds good."

Gillian breathed a deep sigh of relief. She'd accomplished her goal in coming to Del Mar this morning and even gained a date with a man she found incredibly attractive.

As she started to leave the Patio, Carter called out to her. "Gillian?"

She turned around. "Yes?"

"I promise not to let you down."

She smiled and nodded, wishing she could believe him.

Seven

"I can't believe you have a date."

Gillian laughed as she and her best friend, Lily Armbruster, walked into the corner dress shop. "Thanks a lot."

"You know what I mean."

Gillian did know. She hadn't been interested in any man for months. Instead, she'd been focused on her art and the horse sanctuary, telling herself she didn't have time for a relationship. The truth was that something else was holding her back. She wasn't sure if it was the nightmares or simply her dismal history of dating.

Lily stopped to examine a display of purses. "So, tell me about him."

"Well, he's tall, dark and handsome."

"Ah, a T.D.H." Lily said. She liked to use acronyms to categorize men. "That's promising and a lot better than the A.S.S. you usually date?"

"A.S.S.?" Gillian echoed. "As in ass?"

"As in *arrogant, selfish,* and *stupid*. But isn't it funny how the acronym fits that one so perfectly."

She laughed in spite of herself. "Okay, so I've made some bad choices in the past."

"So tell me how this guy is different," Lily challenged her. "Not what he looks like, but how he makes you feel."

It was a dangerous question and one Gillian wasn't sure she wanted to answer. Lily was the kind of friend who didn't pull any punches, a trait which also made her an excellent sculptress. Lily didn't let any critic, even her own inner critic, influence her work.

Her art was raw and gritty and cutting-edge.

The kind of work Gillian wanted to do someday, after she'd made sure Herman wasn't in danger of losing Robards Farm and the sanctuary had plenty of money to support the horses there.

But right now she simply had to play it safe—with her painting and with her heart.

"He makes me feel like I could believe in fairy tales again," Gillian said at last.

"Well, that's a start." Lily put down the lime-green purse she was examining. "So what kind of dress do you want for the ball, Cinderella?"

"Nothing too wild and crazy—I don't want to embarrass the poor man."

"Why not? Then you can see his true character."

"It's one date," Gillian said drily, "not a psychological exam for a permanent boyfriend."

Lily grinned. "Ah, a fling. Even better."

Gillian's face warmed at the thought of a hot and torrid affair with Carter, then she turned her attention to the rack of dresses in front of her. "I want something sophisticated, yet sexy."

Lily pulled out a sleek cocktail dress and held it in front of her. "You can never go wrong with black."

"I want color," Gillian said. "Maybe a print or a solid color. Something bright and vibrant."

She sorted quickly through the dresses in front of her, certain she'd know "the one" when she saw it. At last she pulled out a red halter dress with an hourglass silhouette.

"Oooh, I like it," Lily gushed. "It reminds me of Marilyn Monroe and Audrey Hepburn all rolled up together. Sexy and sophisticated."

Gillian hesitated. "Do you think it sends the wrong message?"

Lily tilted her head to one side. "What message? That you're a single, talented, beautiful twenty-two-year-old woman who's finally ready to cut loose and have a good time?"

"You don't think it says desperate?"

Lily studied her over the top of cat's eye glasses. "Are you desperate?"

That was a loaded question. There were a lot of things happening in her life that made her feel desperate—like her finances and nightmares. But she'd never been desperate for a man, knowing full well that she could only depend on herself.

"No, I'm not desperate." She draped the red dress over her arm. "I'm just a little nervous. The Turf Club Ball is a big deal around here and I might find some potential customers for my portraits. I want to make a good impression on them."

Lily grinned. "Liar."

"Okay," Gillian confessed, laughing. "I am lying. The only person I want to impress is Dr. Carter Phillips. I want to make him so hot for me that he forgets his own name. I want *him* to be desperate."

"That's more like it," Lily chimed. "So go try the dress on while I look for shoes that cost at least half of your last commission. You can't achieve the male desperation effect you want with this guy unless you have the right shoes to go with the dress."

"I'm on a budget," Gillian reminded her.

"So eat soup for the next week. It sound like he'll be worth it."

Lily had a point, but that didn't make money magically appear in her bank account. "I'm only buying shoes that are on sale. I have an appointment with that hypnotherapist to pay for."

Lily's brown eyes widened. "So you're finally going to do it?"

Gillian sighed. "I can't afford not to. Those nightmares are starting to affect my work. I'm too tired to even see straight. Not a good thing for an artist."

Her friend waved off that sentiment. "Depends on the project. Some of them improve with blurry vision, but I know what you mean. I'm just glad you're finally going through with it. I told Christina to expect a call from you."

Lily had been recommending the hypnotherapist for months, but Gillian had been putting it off, determined to beat these nightmares on her own. She'd wrestled with her inner demons before and had always come out on top.

The worst of it had been the survivor guilt she'd suffered after the fire. At ten years old, she didn't think she should laugh again or ever have fun since her parents had died instead of her. Art therapy had helped, as well as several good cries on Herman's shoulder.

Now it was time to vanquish another monster.

Until now, she'd been reluctant to submit to hypnotherapy, as if it meant surrendering to her weakness. Gillian had always found it difficult to face her own flaws. Yet, she'd seen Herman finally admit his gambling addiction and seek help. That had been one of the greatest acts of strength she'd ever witnessed.

"Are you scared to go under hypnosis?" Lily asked bluntly.

"Terrified," Gillian admitted. "Christina's coming to my house for the sessions. She says it's much easier for her patients to relax if they're in a familiar environment."

"You'll like her," Lily promised. "She's very grounded and intuitive. I think she'll be able to help you."

"I hope so. I need to do something before I go crazy. Although I might already be halfway there."

"What do you mean?"

Gillian hesitated. "Lately, I've had this weird feeling that someone's stalking me."

"Who?"

She shook her head. "That's just it. I haven't the faintest idea. It's probably a figment of my imagination, or more likely, the result of my nightmares. After all, I keep seeing a faceless man in my dreams every night. Is it any wonder that I'm looking over my shoulder during the day to see if he's following me?"

Lily looked concerned. "So you don't think you're in danger?"

"I don't know. I did think someone was following me the other day when I left the Arcano Gallery, but I'm probably just exhausted and paranoid. That's why I finally called Christina. I'm ready to move on with my life."

That was also one of the reasons her date with Carter appealed to her so much. She knew he was only in California for a couple of weeks and that suited her just fine. Until she put her past completely behind her, she couldn't contemplate a future with any man.

"Enough about me," Gillian said. "What are you working on now?"

Lily's face lit up at the question. "Oh, you wait until you see it. I'm sculpting an ear."

"An ear?"

"It's gigantic. I've been doing a lot of anatomical research, so I get it just right. I found this supercute otolaryngologist who's agreed to act as my private consultant."

"I'm impressed that you can pronounce *otolaryngologist* and even more that you found a cute one."

She laughed. "You haven't heard the best part about my sculpture. I'm going to fill the ear canal with wax figures from the music world, like Elvis and Madonna. Isn't that cool?"

"Very cool. I can't wait to see it."

"And I can't wait to see you in that dress." Lily shooed her toward the dressing room. "Now go try it on. We might have to hit a lot more stores to find just the right one and I'm meeting the ear doctor for a cozy lunch at my apartment later today."

"More consulting work."

"He's a very thorough man. I like that about him. I'll bet your veterinarian is thorough, too. He probably has a very gentle touch and knows how to turn on all those sensitive nerve endings…"

"Go look for shoes," Gillian interjected before Lily could go any further.

She walked into a fitting room and tried on the dress. Then she looked at herself for a long time in the full-length mirror. To her surprise, it fit perfectly. It also didn't leave any part of her anatomy to the imagination. She'd definitely be sending Carter a message by wearing this dress.

Then again, she was tired of playing it safe.

Carter arrived at Robards Farm on Saturday night only to find that Gillian wasn't there.

"Sorry." Herman stood inside the doorway wearing in his bathrobe and slippers. "She had a problem with one of the horses at her place and asked if you could meet her there."

"No problem," Carter replied, relief flowing through him that she hadn't stood him up. He'd been worried for the last three days that she would change her mind about going out with him.

He turned around to leave when Herman called him back to the house.

"I was wondering if you'd mind taking a quick look at Ranger. I know you've got a tux on and everything, but I think his limp is getting worse."

"I don't mind at all," Carter said. If he wanted to earn Gillian's trust, helping Herman was one way to do it. Even more importantly, he hated to see any animal suffer. He just hoped he could help.

Herman invited Carter inside the living room, then went in search of his border collie. Carter sat down on the sofa and wondered what the hell he was doing. He'd told himself this date was about getting Gillian to trust him, but the way his heart was pounding right now gave lie to that motivation.

He couldn't wait to see her again—couldn't wait to hold her in his arms while they danced. Carter was playing with fire and he knew it. She was too young for him and yet he couldn't stop thinking about her. For the first time in his life, his heart was overruling his head. Carter prided himself on his control, but this passion he had for her was spinning out of control. He knew she couldn't unleash it with one look…one touch.

Carter took a deep breath and tried to gather himself. He needed to put his responsibilities to Quest before his own desires. And he needed to protect Gillian. The last thing he wanted was to become a bad memory for her.

A few minutes later, Herman reappeared in the foyer with a black-and-white dog in his arms. The border collie wagged it tail, but when Herman gently placed him on the ground, the animal lifted his left rear leg and emitted a mournful whimper.

"Hey, there, guy," Carter said, squatting down to examine him. "What seems to be the problem?"

Carter moved slowly, not wanting to startle the dog. Injured animals would often bite or scratch in reaction to pain. He didn't want to do anything to make the border collie's discomfort worse. So he gently palpated the area around the dog's hip, moving his fingers downward until he reached the swollen paw.

His review of Ranger's file hadn't revealed any structural or genetic abnormalities, which led him to his diagnosis. "It looks like he has an infection. There's quite a bit of swelling and he feels warm to the touch. Probably has a slight fever."

"So it's not just a muscle strain?" Herman said.

"No," Carter replied, wishing he'd checked the dog on his first visit.

"How did he get an infection?"

Carter patted the dog on the head, then straightened up to his full height. "Well, I noticed some puncture weeds along the driveway on my way up to the house. It's possible he got a burr in one of his foot pads and that led to the infection."

"Is there anything I can do to make Ranger feel better?"

Carter nodded. "Give him an aspirin tonight to help the fever and relieve the pain. You can wrap the aspirin up in a piece of cheese to make it more palatable to him. Then I'll bring some antibiotic salve over tomorrow that you can apply to the foot pad three times a day. It should heal up fairly quickly."

Herman reached out to shake his hand. "Thank you, Carter. I appreciate it."

"No problem."

Herman walked Carter out to his rented silver Lexus. "I have to say I was surprised to hear Gillian agreed to go on a date with you tonight. The last time I saw the two of you together, it got a little heated."

That was an understatement. "I was surprised, too, but I'm glad she's giving me a second chance."

Herman stopped next to the car. "I'm not one to meddle in my goddaughter's life. Fact is, I don't have much right to ask you not to hurt her when my gambling has hurt her plenty." He arched a silver brow. "Did she tell you about that?"

Carter nodded. "She mentioned it."

Herman tugged at the tie on his robe. "The thing you need to know is that Gillian is sensitive. She may act tough, like she did the day she threw you out of the house, but she's better at protecting other people and animals than she is at protecting herself."

"I won't hurt her," Carter assured him.

Herman's gaze narrowed on him. "Maybe not intentionally. I don't know how long you plan to stick around here, but don't make her any promises you can't keep."

Carter nodded, wondering if Herman sensed that he still wanted—no, needed—to get that DNA test for Picture of Perfection. He wouldn't hurt Gillian to do it, but if he could just convince her…

Now wasn't the time to worry about it. They needed to get to know each other better first, so she'd realize he wasn't a threat to her.

"I guess I've done my fatherly duty," Herman said. "But make no mistake, I will do anything to protect Gillian. Anything."

Carter knew he meant what he said and admired the man for it, even if it did come across as a veiled threat. He understood about protecting the people you loved. His parents and brother meant the world to him. There wasn't anything he wouldn't do for his family. It was part of living up to your responsibilities as a man, something he took very seriously.

"Good night, Herman," Carter said, holding out his hand. "I'll bring out that salve for Ranger in the morning."

"I appreciate it," Herman replied, shaking his hand. "And I'm sure you'll bring my goddaughter back home tonight."

Carter didn't reply as he climbed into the Lexus and drove away. There was protecting someone, then there was overprotecting them. Gillian was twenty-two years old and had surely spent a night away from home before.

Not that he planned to sleep with her on their first date. He'd thought about it, of course. Thought about it way too much in the last three days. But at this moment, all he wanted to do was see her again. He couldn't wait to make her laugh and gaze into those mesmerizing green eyes while they danced.

He turned out of the long driveway and followed Herman's directions to Gillian's ranch. It was a winding gravel road that kicked up a plume of dust behind his shiny car. A herd of horses grazed in a pasture adjacent to the long driveway.

As Carter pulled into the yard, he saw a stable, a corral and a small cottage on the ranch, but nothing else. Only a few concrete blocks remained where the house had once stood, leaving a barren reminder of

Gillian's loss. He was surprised the area hadn't been cleaned up and either rebuilt or at least landscaped.

Now that Herman had gambled away most of her inheritance, he supposed there wasn't enough money left. It told him a lot about Gillian that her first priority had been creating a home for abandoned horses rather than rebuilding what she had lost.

He shifted the car into Park, then climbed out, searching for some sign of her. He saw movement in the corral and headed in that direction.

When he got there, Carter found Gillian leading a horse slowly around the circle of the corral. It only took one glance at her for Carter to realize that he was in serious danger.

If he wasn't careful, Gillian Cameron could lead him anywhere she wanted to go.

Eight

He took a long moment just to drink in the sight of Gillian, amazed at how the woman could have such a profound effect on him. She wore a full-length, body-hugging red dress that revealed every luscious curve of her figure. Her chestnut hair was drawn up into an elegant French knot with just a few stray curls escaping around her long, slender neck.

And she wore cowboy boots. A pair of dusty brown cowboy boots that looked as though they'd seen their fair share of weather and wear. The combination of those cowboy boots and that killer dress made Carter so hot he wondered if he was losing his mind.

As he reached the corral fence, she spotted him and waved. Then she led the Appaloosa over to him.

"Sorry about making us late. Daisy here has a mild case of colic and the trainer had to make a telephone call, so I offered to walk her until he got back."

Carter cleared his throat, trying to play it cool. "I don't mind at all. This way we can make an entrance at the ball."

"You look wonderful," she said, her gaze flicking over his tuxedo.

"So do you."

She laughed. "Yes, I can just imagine the kind of entrance we'd make if I wore these cowboy boots onto the parquet dance floor. Don't worry, though, I have shoes to match the dress. They just wouldn't hold up well in a dusty corral."

Carter climbed over the fence to check on the horse. The young filly looked healthy enough, but he knew the severity of colic could be deceiving.

"Have you taken her temperature?"

"Yes, it's normal," Gillian said. "So is her pulse and respiration."

Carter was impressed. "Sounds like you know what you're doing."

"Ian knows more about horses than I ever will," she explained. "He was the trainer on our ranch before the fire and just moved back here a few months ago when I asked him to train Picture of Perfection. I'm lucky he agreed to come out of retirement."

"So he's the man helping you with the sanctuary horses, too?"

She nodded. "In exchange for living in the cottage, since I can't pay him much of a salary yet. Fortunately, he's got a lot of confidence in Picture of Perfection's future, so he was nice enough to defer the kind of salary he deserves."

Carter decided that, despite her confidence in Ian's abilities, he'd give the young Appaloosa a quick exam to make sure the colic wasn't more serious than they suspected.

"What has her appetite been like in the past day or so?" he asked.

"Ian told me she's grazed a little, but is off her feed."

"Has Daisy suffered any diarrhea or constipation?"

"No."

Carter walked around to the front of the horse. "How about her water intake?"

"According to Ian, she's been drinking about the right amount of water. Not too much or too little."

Carter grasped her bridle, then eased open the filly's mouth to check the color of her gums. He was relieved to see they looked normal.

"What's your diagnosis, Dr. Phillips?"

He turned to look at her, trying not to stare at the generous amount of cleavage revealed by the halter top of her dress. "Perfect. I mean, your treatment seems perfect so far. Walking is good for her and helps to keep her distracted from the pain. Just make sure she's not walked to the point of exhaustion."

Carter heard a disdainful snort behind him.

"Like I would ever do such a foolish thing."

He turned around to see a grizzled old cowboy hanging on the corral fence. With an agility that belied his age, the man hopped over the fence and took the reins of the Appaloosa from Gillian.

"I can take over here now, hon. You go on to your dance."

Gillian made the introductions. "Ian, this is Dr. Carter Phillips. Carter, this is Ian Wiley, the best trainer in California and uncle to Picture of Perfection's jockey, Finn Wiley. I've known Ian forever."

Ian grinned at her. "I was always having to chase you out of the stable when you were little and look at you now, all dressed up like some kind of movie star. Too bad you've got horse manure on your boots."

"I do not," she exclaimed, looking down at her footwear.

"Okay, maybe you don't," Ian teased. "Now, why don't you trade those boots in for those fancy high heels so you don't keep your date waiting any longer."

"I don't mind," Carter said.

Ian scowled at him. "Well, I do. I've got work to do around here and you two are holding me up."

Gillian leaned over to kiss his cheek. "I'll see you tomorrow, Ian."

Ian's face softened. "Have a good time tonight, Gilly."

"Gilly?" Carter echoed as they walked toward the stable.

She blushed. "It's what everyone used to call me when I was little and Ian's just never gotten out of the habit. I guess I'm used to it."

"I like it." He watched her sit down on a straw bale and pull off her cowboy boots. Her bare feet were pale and perfect, with bright red polish on her toenails that matched her dress.

She pulled a pair of red heels from a bag, then slipped her feet into them, adding a good three inches to her height.

"Wow," he breathed.

She smiled. "They're definitely an improvement over the boots."

Carter knew that he'd have the same reaction to her no matter what she wore. Gillian had a sensuality about her that was almost palpable.

"Is something wrong?" Her brow crinkled as she looked up at him.

He swallowed hard, reminding himself that he was going to take it slow even if it killed him. "No, I'm fine. Are you ready?"

"Let's go."

He led her to the Lexus and held the door open for her, aware of Ian watching them every step of the way. It seemed as if Herman wasn't the only man in her life with an overprotective streak. Both of them displayed a paternal love for her that was hard to miss.

Carter started the car, eager for them to be on their way. Tonight, he wanted Gillian all to himself.

When they arrived at the hotel ballroom, the party was already in full swing. A band entertained the crowd with lively music and waiters circulated around the room with trays of appetizers and champagne.

Gillian could feel Carter's hand lightly grasping her elbow, as if he was afraid to lose her in the throng. She'd been pleased by his reaction to the dress and didn't even regret the amount of money she'd spent on the shoes. His expression was well worth the penny-pinching she'd have to do for the next several weeks to make up for it.

"There's our table," Carter said, leading her toward the far corner of the room. She recognized the cute blonde named Melanie, but not the man seated beside her. Gillian hoped that was Melanie's date.

"Hey, there," Melanie greeted them as they approached. "I thought you'd never get here."

"One of Gillian's young fillies is suffering through a bout of colic."

Concern filled Melanie's eyes, boosting up Gillian's opinion of her several notches. "Nothing too serious, I hope."

"I think she'll be fine," Gillian replied, taking the seat that Carter held out for her. "At least, Carter seems to think so."

"Well, he is the best vet in the business," Melanie affirmed, then turned to the man on her left. "This is Marcus Vasquez, the head trainer for Quest Stables. Marcus, this is Gillian Cameron."

Marcus stood up and held out his hand. "Nice to meet you."

She shook his hand, admiring his Spanish accent even as she wondered how Melanie knew her name. Carter hadn't introduced them to each other at the Del Mar racetrack. Obviously he'd told Melanie about Gillian after she'd left, but what exactly had he said?

"How about a glass of champagne?" Carter offered as a waiter approached their table.

"Yes, please," Gillian replied, trying to ignore the uneasiness stirring inside of her.

"I saw your painting of Picture of Perfection," Melanie told her. "You've got great talent. It's like the horse comes alive on the canvas."

"Thank you." Gillian lifted the champagne glass to her lips. Maybe this wasn't a real date after all, but a tag-team effort by Quest Stables employees to convince her to run a blood test on Picture of Perfection.

Her gaze shifted to Marcus, who didn't seem to be following the conversation. Although he was a handsome man with dark hair and even darker eyes, his face was pinched with tension and he kept looking at his watch.

Carter turned to Melanie. "Where's your brother this evening?"

She shrugged. "He was supposed to be here half an hour ago, but I haven't seen him yet."

Marcus abruptly rose to his feet. "Excuse me, please."

Gillian watched him go, then realized she wasn't the only one surprised by his sudden departure.

"What's up with him?" Melanie asked Carter.

He shook his head. "I don't know. I heard Robbie disagreeing with Marcus about the training method for one of the horses today. Maybe they still haven't worked it out."

Melanie sighed. "What were my parents thinking when they picked Marcus over my brother for head trainer? I mean, Marcus is a wonderful trainer and a great guy, but now Robbie thinks he has to prove himself all the time. It's just a mess."

Gillian sat back in her chair, wondering if the entire evening was going to consist of Quest Stables business. It seemed to her that with the scandal involving Leopold's Legacy, they had more important problems than who should be head trainer. Then again, she knew how easy it was for trouble to spread. Like ripples in a pond, it could affect everything and everyone it touched.

She looked over at Carter, wondering how the scandal had touched him. Despite Melanie's confidence in his abilities, his job might be at stake if the paternity issue involving Leopold's Legacy wasn't resolved before a ban on all the stable's horses took place. Herman had filled Gillian in on the details and she knew Quest Stables was in a very precarious position. They could lose everything.

Gillian sat up in her chair, girding herself against the empathy welling inside of her. She knew all too well what it was like to face imminent ruin. At this point in her life, she simply couldn't afford to let her sympathy for the people at Quest derail any of her plans. Herman depended on her and so did all those abandoned horses at her ranch.

"Gillian?"

She blinked, then looked up at Carter, realizing too late that he had been speaking to her. "Oh, I'm sorry. I guess I was lost in my thoughts."

"I don't blame you," Melanie chimed as she rose from the table. "I've been monopolizing the conversation with all of this Quest Stables talk that I'm sure is of no interest to you."

The words stung, implying a callousness that Gillian was certain Melanie hadn't meant. "Oh, I wouldn't say that."

Melanie flashed a smile. "Well, that's very kind of you. I'm going to mingle and get my mind off work for a change. You two have fun."

When they were alone at the table, Carter turned to Gillian. "Did I happen to mention how beautiful you look tonight?"

"I think so—" she placed her chin in her hand and leaned toward him "—but I certainly wouldn't mind hearing it again."

He smiled. "You look...amazing."

"Go on."

His smile widened. "I've also noticed I'm not the only man in the room who can't seem to take his eyes off you."

Her green eyes narrowed. "Now you're exaggerating, Carter."

"Not at all," he countered, rising to his feet. "In fact, I see my good friend Troy headed this way, so I'm going to ask you to dance before I have to introduce you to him."

"Is he that bad?"

"Yes. Definitely not the kind of guy a lady can trust."

"And you are?" she asked as they moved toward the dance floor.

"Always." Carter pulled her into his arms and Gillian swallowed a gasp at the sensation of his tall, hard body against her own. All her uneasiness faded as she molded herself against him. It almost felt as if this was exactly where she was meant to be.

Careful, she warned herself, knowing her tendency to fall too hard and too quickly. Just because Carter had said she could trust him didn't make it true. But she was also tired of living a life of caution. Maybe Lily was right and she just needed a wild fling.

"You're very quiet," he said into her ear, his breath a tingling caress that reached Gillian all the way down to her toes.

She suppressed a shiver of delight as she moved

even closer to him. "I'm just enjoying the dance. It's been a long time since I had such a good partner."

"Me, too."

Gillian lifted her head to meet his gaze. "Where did you learn to dance like this?"

He sighed. "My mother was a ballroom dance instructor for years and I was the obligatory partner whenever a single woman took the class."

"Really?"

He nodded. "I grew up in South Chicago. We lived in an apartment above my mother's studio. My father worked as a salesman, so he was gone a lot."

"Then you must have some great moves."

He grinned. "So I've been told."

Gillian could only imagine. She knew dancing was a symbolic mating ritual for many cultures, and if the way Carter moved on the dance floor resembled the way he moved in bed...

She shook that thought from her head, realizing this wasn't the time or the place for that kind of fantasy. "So tell me more about your family."

"They're still in Chicago," he said wistfully. "My younger brother will be starting his junior year at Northwestern."

"Does your mother still teach ballroom dancing?"

"No." His voice tightened, "She can barely walk anymore. She has multiple sclerosis."

"Oh, Carter, I'm sorry. That must be so hard for all of you."

"It is." Pain and regret cast a shadow in his blue eyes. "Although my mom handles it amazingly well and my father just found a new job that keeps him in Chicago so he can take care of her."

"Is it hard for you to live so far away from them?"

"More than I want to admit sometimes. I go back whenever I can. Fortunately, even with my mom's illness, she's still pretty independent."

"That's good." She laid her head on his shoulder. "I'm sure they're very proud of you."

He didn't say anything and Gillian sensed that there was more that Carter wasn't telling her. As the music ended, she wondered if she should push the issue or simply ask him for another dance.

His grasp tightened on her and she looked up in surprise. He was staring toward the door.

"What's wrong?" she asked.

"I think I see trouble."

Nine

Carter headed toward the entrance to the ballroom with Gillian trailing right behind him. Robbie and Marcus stood just outside the door, their faces flushed and their voices growing louder.

"I won't be undermined by you or anyone," Marcus said firmly.

Fury flashed in Robbie's eyes as he took a menacing step toward him. "And I won't sit back and shut up when I see mistakes being made."

"Get out of my face." Marcus's voice was a low growl and Carter picked up his pace.

"If you don't like it here, you're more than welcome to leave."

"I'm not going anywhere," Marcus retorted. "So get used to it."

Just as Robbie swung his fist back, Carter grabbed his arm and held it there.

"Not here and not now," he warned in a low voice. "Quest has enough problems without you two starting a brawl at the Turf Club Ball."

His words seemed to have the effect he intended. Both men stepped apart from each other, as if finally realizing they were the center of attention in the ballroom.

"Why don't you go outside and cool off," Carter suggested to the youngest Preston.

"Good idea." Robbie turned on his heel and strode away.

Marcus straightened his jacket. "Sorry, Carter. I guess my temper got the better of me. I know he wants my job, but I won't let him sabotage me to get it."

"Robbie would never sabotage Quest Stables," Carter assured him. "He's just stubborn and wants to prove himself."

"At my expense." Marcus glanced over Carter's shoulder at Gillian. "Please forgive my behavior, Ms. Cameron. It's been a little tense around here lately."

"I understand," Gillian replied. "There's nothing to forgive."

"Thank you," Marcus said. "I think I'll turn in for the night."

Carter breathed a sigh of relief that the situation

had been so easily defused. That confrontation was just one more sign that Quest Stables was nearing the breaking point. Everyone was under pressure and they had to find an outlet somewhere. He was just sorry it had happened in front of so many of Quest's competitors.

He watched Marcus walk away, relieved to see him go in a direction opposite Robbie's. Hopefully, both men would walk off their anger and put it behind them by morning. Horses could sense that kind of emotion and it would only lead to trouble on the track if it continued.

Gillian's slender hand curled around his arm. "Are you all right?"

He swallowed a sigh. "Yes, I'm fine. Sorry about that."

She smiled. "Hey, it's not often I get a date who's a ballroom dancer *and* can break up an impending fight without throwing a punch. Where did you learn that particular skill?"

His mood lightened. "Veterinary school. When two males, human or animal, are fighting for the same territory, it can lead to a lot of trouble."

"And what happens when it's a male and a female?"

Her tone made him forget about Marcus and Robbie and focus completely on her. "That's another situation entirely, but it can be just as dangerous."

"Really?" She moved a step closer to him, her lips only a few tantalizing inches away.

Carter's hands found their way to her hips and he pulled her even closer, not able to resist temptation any longer.

"Excuse me," said a soft voice behind him. "Dr. Phillips, is that you?"

He swallowed a groan of frustration, then turned around to see a familiar woman with a shy smile on her face.

"It's me, Shirley," she exclaimed. "Shirley Biden, from the auction. Remember?"

"Of course I remember you, Mrs. Biden," he replied. "It's nice to see you again."

"And so very nice to see you." She clasped her hands together in delight. "I almost feel like a matchmaker since I'm the one who set up the auction."

She turned her attention to Gillian. "You're the artist, right? The one who painted the portrait of that magnificent horse. I saw your name in the paper just this morning in an advertisement for an exhibit at the Arcano Gallery. It's Gillian, isn't it? Gillian Cameron?"

"That's right," Gillian said cordially. "It's nice to meet you."

"And so very nice to meet you," Shirley replied. "I talked to your godfather on the phone the other day to set up the appointment with Dr. Phillips. He was the nicest man. Herman, wasn't it?"

"Yes," Gillian replied, a twinkle of amusement lighting her green eyes. "He is a very nice man."

"I thought so. You can always tell so much about a

person from their voice." She beamed at them. "So, when did you two start dating?"

Gillian glanced up at Carter. "Well, I guess you could say this is our first date."

"Oh, how sweet. And you both look so nice."

A new band took the stage and the toe-tapping beat of a Frank Sinatra song floated across the ballroom.

"Listen to that music," Shirley exclaimed, placing a thin hand on her chest. "My husband and I used to love to dance the fox-trot. He passed away five years ago and it's at times like this that I really miss him."

Gillian looked up at Carter and gave him an encouraging smile—the kind of smile that he couldn't refuse.

He turned to Shirley and said, "May I have this dance, Mrs. Biden?"

Her eyes widened. "Why...of course. If you're sure Gillian doesn't mind."

"Not at all," she assured the woman, then looked up at Carter. "I'll get us some more champagne and wait for you in the courtyard."

"I'll be there shortly," he promised, watching her walk away.

"Such a nice young woman," Shirley said with a wistful sigh. "Are you sure you want to dance with me, Dr. Phillips? I won't take offense if you've changed your mind."

Carter smiled down at the woman who had brought Gillian Cameron into his life. "I wouldn't miss it for the world."

* * *

Gillian waited outside on the veranda, the ocean breeze a welcome respite from the warm ballroom. A full moon shone in the sky, bathing the veranda in an ethereal glow. She took a sip of her champagne, setting Carter's glass on the small wrought iron table in front of her.

Music from the ballroom floated outside and a smile came unbidden to Gillian's lips. Carter was giving Mrs. Biden a little piece of her past back—a priceless gift. When he'd invited the older woman to dance, Gillian had been so touched that she thought she might cry.

That's why she was out here instead of watching them on the dance floor. She was falling much too fast and much too hard for Carter and this was only their first date. Possibly their only date, although the way he looked at her made her believe he felt much the same way as she did.

"Excuse me, miss."

She turned around to see a man in an impeccable gray tuxedo make a small bow. "Yes?"

"My name is Troy. Dr. Troy Daley, to be precise. Carter is one of my good friends and I know he wouldn't want me to let his lovely date stand out here all by herself."

She smiled at his flirtatious tone. "That's very kind of you, but I don't mind."

"Then tell me," he said, a wistful grin playing over his mouth, "do you have a twin sister or something because…damn…you look nice."

Her smile widened. "Sorry, I'm an only child."

"Just my luck. How did you and Carter meet anyway? When I saw him walk into the ballroom with you, I just about fell over in my chair. He usually comes stag to these events or prefers to skip them altogether."

"We met after he bought a horse portrait of mine at a local charity auction. Meeting the artist was part of the prize."

Troy nodded. "A prize indeed. Well, if you don't have a twin sister, how about a cute artist friend who wouldn't mind a blind date with a lonely veterinarian?"

Gillian smiled as she imagined pairing him up with Lily. "I'm afraid the only cute artist friend I have is already involved with an otolaryngologist."

He laughed. "Damn, those ear doctors get all the women. I guess I went into the wrong field."

She leaned back against the veranda railing. "So how long have you known Carter?"

He thought for a moment. "Well, it's got to be at least five or six years. We've been on the racing circuit together a long time."

Her mind went back to the earlier confrontation between Robbie and Marcus. "This scandal at Quest is pretty serious, isn't it."

Troy's expression sobered. "Very serious. I don't know what I'd do in Carter's shoes. His reputation as an equine specialist will take a beating if they don't figure out how this happened."

"You don't believe he had anything to do with the problem, do you?"

"Carter?" Troy said in disbelief. "Of course not. He's the very definition of honor. Just look at everything he does for his family, even though…" His voice trailed off and he took another sip of his champagne.

"Even though what?" she prompted.

He shook his head. "I think I've taken up enough of your time."

"I agree," Carter said as he approached them. He didn't look happy to see Troy there.

His friend grinned, not the least intimidated by the scowl on Carter's face. "I was just keeping your date company for you, Carter. I'm sure you'd do the same for me."

"Good night, Troy," he said pointedly.

Troy laughed. "Good night." Then he winked at Gillian. "Wonderful to meet you, Gillian. Tell your friend that if she gets tired of the ear guy I'm available."

When he was gone, Gillian looked up at Carter. "So how was the dance?"

"Nice," he replied. "Mrs. Biden is very light on her feet." He glanced over his shoulder at the retreating Troy. "So what's this about an ear guy?"

She picked up the glass of champagne from the table and handed it to him. "Oh, it's nothing. He wants me to fix him up with one of my friends."

He took a sip of champagne. "And?"

"And she's already involved with someone, for this week anyway."

He set the champagne flute back on the table, then

moved closer to her. His nearness made her shiver with anticipation.

"Cold?"

"Yes," she lied.

He took off his suit coat and laid it over her bare shoulders. It was still warm from his body and the scent of his cologne filled her senses.

"How about you, Gillian? Are you involved with anyone?"

She looked up at him, her heart beating hard in her chest. "No."

He took another step closer, his hands circling around her waist. "Do you want to be?"

She answered him by wrapping her arms around his neck and pulling his mouth down on hers. A low groan rumbled in his throat as she kissed him, and his arms tightened around her.

Kissing Carter Phillips was even better than she had imagined and Gillian had been fantasizing about it all night. She slid her hands from his neck and cupped his face in her palms as the kiss deepened, their tongues engaged in a primal dance.

Her fingers caressed his jaw and she felt the promise of his whiskers just beneath the skin. He was more man than she'd handled in a long time, but Gillian was ready for the experience.

Her body melted against him and her legs felt weak, but she didn't stop kissing him. The music faded away and the jacket suddenly made her feel too warm. She let it drop from her shoulders, wanting every bit of skin-to-skin contact that his hands could provide.

Those hands roamed up over her arms and onto her shoulders, kneading them gently as his mouth softened on hers. The sudden tenderness in his kiss affected her even more than his raw passion had just moments before.

Gillian softly cried out as she pulled away from him, completely unprepared for the emotions suddenly welling inside of her.

Concern mingled with hot flames of desire in his blue eyes. "What's wrong?"

"Nothing," she gasped, struggling to collect herself. "Your jacket fell off."

She bent down to retrieve it, shaken to the core by his kiss and the feelings it had evoked. This didn't feel like a fling. It felt much more powerful. Much more dangerous.

"Carter," she said, finally meeting his gaze. "Please take me home."

Ten

The next day, Carter pulled into Robards Farm, glad he had an excuse to be there. He still didn't understand what the hell had happened last night, but something had made Gillian pull away from him. One moment they were entangled in the hottest kiss he'd ever experienced and the next she was giving off an Arctic chill.

Maybe he'd pushed her too fast, although she'd been the one to initiate that kiss. He still couldn't forget the way she'd felt in his arms or how he'd wanted that kiss to lead to something more. They'd been headed in that direction when Gillian had slammed on the brakes. Maybe that was a good thing, since he couldn't seem to control himself around her. All his good intentions to play it safe had vanished almost as soon as he'd seen her last night.

Carter parked his car next to a green Subaru he didn't recognize, then he grabbed his canvas medical bag. As he walked toward the house, he thought about the first time he'd seen Picture of Perfection standing alone in the pasture.

He was still struck by the horse's incredible likeness to Leopold's Legacy. The two stallions not only looked the same, but could both run like the wind. He'd love to see Picture of Perfection race in the Pacific Classic.

Even better would be watching him with Gillian at his side. The way she had retreated from him last night made the possibility of that happening look more remote than ever.

Carter slung his medical bag over his shoulder and stepped onto the front porch. He knocked on the door, but there was no answer. After waiting a few moments, he knocked again. Herman was expecting him with the salve, so someone had to be here.

Then he heard Gillian scream.

Without hesitation, he reached for the doorknob, relieved to find that it turned easily in his hand. Then he was inside the house, his heart racing as he hurried to find Gillian.

Another agonizing cry led him into the living room. That's when he saw her lying on the sofa, her green eyes open and filled with panic. She was coughing, almost choking, and her hands were outstretched in front of her as if she was reaching for something she couldn't see.

A woman he hadn't noticed before sat in a wing chair, looking unfazed by Gillian's obvious distress. She was tall, close to six feet, with straight blond hair and hazel eyes. She didn't see him standing in the doorway; her entire focus was on Gillian.

His gaze turned back to her and he watched Gillian claw at the sofa, her breath coming in deep, ragged gasps that made his own chest hurt.

"Gillian," the woman said, her voice clear and calm. "I want you to start walking backward, back toward the bed in your old room. The smoke is clearing now. You're able to breathe as time is moving backward, faster and faster. You're in bed now, your blankets are tucked in all around you, keeping you safe."

Carter's gut tightened when he realized she was undergoing some type of hypnosis and reliving the fire that had killed her parents. He wondered why she would put herself through such torment, especially when it had happened so many years ago.

He stood rooted to the spot, his medical bag slipping off his shoulder and falling silently onto the thick carpet. Carter didn't want to interrupt Gillian's session, but he couldn't leave, either. Not until he knew that she was all right.

Gillian was quieter now, her cries for help replaced

by small, heart-wrenching sobs. Her face looked pale, and her eyes were wide-open and searching for something she couldn't seem to find.

He watched as the fear on her face gradually began to recede and her arms stilled on the sofa. Her breathing grew less frantic and tortured as her eyes started drifting closed.

"You're asleep in your bed," hypnotherapist intoned, leaning forward. "You're warm and safe there. Now I want you to go back in time some more. I want you to see yourself before you fall asleep. Pretend that you're floating above your body and just tell me everything that you see yourself doing. And I want you to remember that nothing can hurt you. You're warm and safe."

Gillian dragged in a deep breath, then said, "I'm getting out of bed and tiptoeing toward the door. I don't want my mom and dad to hear me."

Her voice sounded different to his ears. Like that of a child. His heart contracted when he thought of how she'd gone though such a tragic event at such a young age. Only ten years old.

"Why don't you want your parents to hear you," the woman asked her.

"Because they'll make me go back to bed," Gillian said. "I want to watch the movie. It's really scary and Tommy Williams said I'd be too scared to watch it, so I have to prove him wrong."

Carter smiled at the indignation he heard in her

voice. Even at ten, Gillian wasn't going to let anyone call her a coward. Then again, she'd had to be tough to endure everything she'd gone through.

In his mind, she'd demonstrated her indomitable courage in almost every facet of her life. Like pursuing an art career—a move many would call risky. She'd also opened the horse sanctuary—an endeavor that cost money rather than earned it. She was even trying to pull Herman out of the deep financial hole he'd dug for himself and fighting to protect their interests in Picture of Perfection.

"Tell me what you are doing now, Gillian," the hypnotherapist prompted her.

Gillian's eyes were closed as she spoke. "I'm opening my bedroom door very slowly so it won't squeak. I'm holding Morris carefully because I don't want him to squeak, either."

Carter tensed as he listened to her. It took every bit of strength he had not to go to her and pull her into his arms. To hold her until all her pain went away. He knew he was intruding on her privacy, but he simply couldn't make himself leave

"I'm walking down the stairs to the living room," Gillian continued. "It's dark, but I don't want to turn on the light."

Her voice is tighter now and her eyes glazed with apprehension.

"You're safe," the hypnotherapist reminded her. "You're floating in the air and nothing can hurt you there. You're just watching everything happen from far away, like in a movie."

Gillian moistened her lips with her tongue. "I turn on the television set, but I worry that if I turn it up too loud, Mom and Dad will hear it. So I decide to lie down on the floor right in front of it so I only have to turn it up just a little bit."

Carter watched her visibly shiver. He'd never witnessed a hypnotherapy session before and was mesmerized by how deeply Gillian seemed to be entranced.

"I'm really cold," Gillian said, folding her hands over her arms. "The movie's about to start, but I need a blanket."

The way she spoke, Carter could almost see the scene in his mind. He pictured a young, ten-year-old Gillian, clad in pajamas with a teddy bear clasped under one arm. The muted green glow of the television the only light in the room.

"There's a blanket on the sofa," Gillian continued. "And I see a candle on the coffee table. Maybe I won't be scared if I have light from the candle."

Carter closed his eyes, fearing what she was going to say next.

"There's a lighter by the candle. I have to flick it twice before it works. Then I light the candle. It smells like jasmine."

"What happens after you light the candle?" the hypnotherapist asked her.

"I lay down in front of the television. Me and Morris

are under the blanket. I put it over my head during the scary parts of the movie. I'm so sleepy…."

Her voice started to fade and Carter saw her body sink even farther into the sofa.

"Gillian?" the hypnotherapist said softly. "I'm going to count to three, and when I snap my fingers, you're going to wake up. You'll feel safe and rested and comfortable. One…two…three."

At the snap of the woman's fingers, Gillian's eyes opened. She rose slowly to a sitting position, looking a little disoriented.

"How do you feel?" Christina asked her.

Gillian rubbed a hand over her face. "Fine." Then she turned and saw Carter standing in the doorway and her eyes widened in dismay. "What are you doing here?"

Gillian didn't understand what was going on. She felt more rested than she had in months, yet still a little fuzzy about what had just happened.

"I heard you scream," Carter told her. "I thought you were in some kind of trouble, so I just ran inside to help you."

Christina turned at the sound of his voice, a frown on her face. "You've been standing there the whole time?"

"Most of it," he admitted. "I'm sorry, I didn't mean to intrude."

The thought of Carter watching her during the

therapy session made Gillian uncomfortable. She wished she could remember everything she'd said and done.

Closing her eyes for a moment, she let herself relax. Then it all came flooding back. The sight of her sneaking downstairs to watch a horror flick on television. Taking Morris with her so she wouldn't be afraid. Grabbing the blanket off the sofa.

Lighting the candle.

Christina turned back to Gillian. "I'm sorry. I didn't know he was there."

"It's all right," she said, feeling a little numb. "This is Dr. Carter Phillips. He's a friend. Carter, this is Christina Conway, a certified hypnotherapist."

They nodded at each other, though both of them were keeping their attention on Gillian.

"You did very well for your first session," Christina told her. "It's very important that we go slowly so that your emotions don't block any of those buried memories."

Gillian gave her a silent nod.

"Do you have any questions for me?" Christina asked her.

Gillian shook her head, too unnerved to say a single word.

Christina rose to her feet, seemingly unconcerned about her client's silence. Gillian found herself wondering if all the woman's clients had this kind of reaction to their first hypnosis session, especially if it involved a traumatic event.

"I'll leave you now." Christina picked up the striped knit bag at her feet. "It's going to take some time for you to process what's happened. Don't come to any conclusions just yet. We still have a lot of work to do."

Gillian nodded, fearing they'd already uncovered the only memory that really mattered.

Christina's gaze softened on her. "What you remembered during that session is an old memory that's been buried deep in your mind for a long time. You need to give yourself time to absorb it so other memories can come through. Right now, that memory is like pulling a page out of a century-old book and placing it in the middle of a brand-new one. You have to look at it in context."

Carter didn't move from the doorway and Gillian didn't have the inner strength to ask him to leave. She didn't *want* him to leave—not when she was feeling so alone and afraid and vulnerable.

"Please don't hesitate to call me if you have any questions or concerns before our next session," Christina told her, then she reached over to pat Gillian's hand. "You'll be all right, Gillian. I'm here to help you through all of this."

She watched the therapist move past Carter and out the front door, leaving her alone in the house with him. He didn't say anything for a long moment. Then walked over to the sofa.

"You never told me you were in the house," he said, kneeling down beside her. "I had no idea that you'd almost died in that fire, too."

"Ian saved me," she told him. "Not that I remember it, that's just what I was told. I didn't remember much of anything from that night."

"That's why you're undergoing hypnosis?"

She nodded. "To get my memories back."

One memory she'd never forget was that kiss they'd shared last night. Gillian met his gaze, remembering how wonderful he'd made her feel. So wonderful it had scared her half to death. She'd promised herself not to see him again—yet, here he was in her living room. Worst of all, he'd heard the truth about her—a truth she still didn't want to face.

"Gillian," he said softly. "Are you sure you're all right?"

She looked into his kind blue eyes and something melted inside of her. "I did it," she whispered. "I started the fire that killed my parents."

The next moment she was in his arms, a sob of anguish rising up in her throat that she couldn't seem to stop. She regretted ever hiring Christina, ever finding out the truth. Her amnesia surrounding the circumstances of the fire had been a blessing in disguise.

"You don't know that you started the fire," Carter told her when she finally pulled away from him. "It didn't come out during the session. All you did was light a candle."

"Ian told me he found me at the bottom of the stairs. I always thought I'd gotten there from my bedroom." She swallowed another sob, trying not to fall completely apart in front of him. "In my nightmares, I'm always in my bedroom trying to find the door. Now I know I was never there. That's probably why I got out of the house when my parents didn't make it, because I was on the first floor when Ian found me."

Carter brushed a tear off her cheek. "Listen to me. You don't know everything that happened yet. During the session, you were talking about feeling sleepy while you were watching television. Then you seemed to fall asleep, so that's where Christina stopped the session. You don't know what happened next."

He was right, but it gave her little comfort. A burning candle seemed like the most obvious reason for the fire, yet the cause had been reported as undetermined.

She rubbed a hand over her temple. "I don't know what to think."

"How long have you been having nightmares about the fire?" he asked gently. "Ever since it happened?"

She shook her head. "No, that's what's so strange about all of this. The nightmares just started about six months ago. I have no idea what triggered them after all of this time."

Carter thought for a moment. "Can you connect it to any recent change in your life?"

She gave a small shrug. "Well, in the last six months, I've graduated from art school, hired Ian back to train Picture of Perfection and caught the attention of an art gallery owner who wants to give me my own showing."

Amusement shone in Carter's eyes. "So, nothing much, then."

She smiled in spite of herself. "I guess my life is changing a little."

"It's changing a lot," he replied. "Just like your life changed a lot after the fire. Maybe that's why you started having the nightmares, because your subconscious somehow linked all the changes in your life back to that fire."

She tilted her head to one side. "Are you sure you're a veterinarian and not a psychologist?"

He shook his head. "Sorry for the amateur analysis. I just want to help."

She rose to her feet, feeling the need to move. An urge to run rushed through her, to run as fast and as far as she could go. Instead, she paced the length of the living room floor, hoping to release all this restless energy inside of her.

"You still haven't explained why you came here today," she said.

He rose to his feet. "I told Herman I'd bring some antibiotic salve for his dog. He's got an infection in his foot."

She nodded. "So that's why Ranger's been limping around."

"Yes."

"I wish there was a salve that could help me. I don't want to do this anymore, Carter. I don't want to remember anything else."

He moved in front of her, making it impossible for her to keep pacing. "You're in charge of your own life, Gillian. You aren't controlled by the past, or by memories, or by nightmares. There's nothing to fear."

She looked up into his eyes. "Isn't there?"

In that moment, she knew they were both thinking about the kiss they'd shared and where it would have led if she'd let things take their natural course. If she hadn't stopped him, Gillian knew they would have spent the night very differently.

Now she wanted to feel that spark of desire again—to feel anything but the fear and trepidation that had tied her up in knots.

"Not from me," he said. "You have nothing to fear from me."

She reached up to touch his face, her fingertips caressing the length of his jaw. "Oh, how I want to believe that. You'll never know how much."

"Gillian," he breathed, then leaned down to kiss her.

Eleven

It was a gentle kiss, a balm meant to soothe and comfort, but they both wanted more. She circled her arms around his neck as he pulled her closer, pressing her soft body tightly against his own.

He groaned low in his throat and the passion that had flared between them last night sparked once more.

Then he heard the front door open and the sound of Herman's dog barking. Forcing himself to pull away, he broke the kiss. Gillian took a step back, her hand coming up to her mouth.

"Has anyone ever told your godfather he has lousy timing?" he asked.

She blushed. "But you came here to see him, didn't you?"

Before he could reply, Herman walked into the living room, the border collie limping behind him.

Herman's brown eyes widened when he saw the two of them together. "Am I interrupting anything?"

"Not at all." Gillian walked over and kissed his cheek. "I have some work to do upstairs, so I'll leave you two alone."

"Gillian," Carter called after her, not certain what to say. Especially with Herman standing there.

She turned around. "Yes?"

"Do you still want me to bring the portrait to the art gallery this week?"

"Yes," she replied. "Will Monday afternoon work for you? As the owner, you have to sign a legal release giving the Arcano Gallery permission to display it."

He didn't care about legal papers, he just wanted to know when he would see her again. "Will you be there?"

"I will," she said, a blush suffusing her cheeks. "I have an appointment with the owner at two o'clock."

"Good. Then I'll see you then."

Without another word, Gillian turned on her heel and hurried up the stairs. Carter watched her, wondering what she was thinking—if she was regretting that second kiss between them. Maybe he'd taken advantage of her at a vulnerable moment. If so, he didn't regret it. He'd never regret kissing Gillian.

Herman cleared his throat. "I get the feeling there was something I missed."

Carter turned around and picked up the medical bag off the floor. "I walked in during Gillian's hypnotherapy session. It shook her up quite a bit."

Herman paled. "Her what?"

Carter realized too late that Gillian might not have shared her plans with her godfather. "You should probably talk to her about it."

"I'd rather talk to you," Herman said bluntly. "Now tell me what this is all about."

Carter opened his medical bag, shuffling through the contents for the tube of antibiotic salve that he'd brought for the dog. He wasn't sure it was his place to tell Herman about the session, but he could reveal just enough to make it clear that Gillian was in a vulnerable state.

"She's been having nightmares about the fire that killed her parents."

"I know about that part," he said. "Sometimes I hear her cry out."

"I guess she hired a hypnotherapist to help her figure out what's causing those nightmares so she can stop them."

Herman didn't say anything as Carter picked up the border collie and set him on his lap. Opening the tube of salve, he applied a generous amount to the dog's swollen foot pad, then did a quick exam to make certain the infection was still localized.

"Ranger looks a little better than he did yesterday," Carter observed, scratching the dog behind his ears.

"He acts better, too," Herman said. "Though he's still limping."

"The limp should gradually get better once the salve starts working. Keep giving him the aspirin every day and let me know if his condition changes for the worse."

"Thanks. I appreciate it." Herman took the dog from him, along with the salve.

Carter sensed a tension in the air that hadn't been there before. He didn't know if Herman had seen him kissing Gillian or if he was upset that he hadn't been told about the hypnotherapy session. Whatever the reason, it was time for him to leave.

"I'll walk you out," Herman said as he watched Carter pack up his bag.

"That's not necessary. I know the way."

"I insist."

Carter looked up at the man and was surprised to see the flash of anger in his brown eyes. He slung the bag over his shoulder and headed for the door, ready to face the confrontation he knew was about to come.

Herman barely waited until the front door was closed behind them before he spoke. "What the hell do you think you're doing?"

Carter turned around. "What do you mean?"

"You know damn well what I mean. Coming here and kicking up trouble in Gillian's life. She never mentioned seeing a hypno-whatever until she met you."

"I had nothing to do with that," Carter retorted. "I stumbled into her session by accident when I heard her scream. Why is it a problem, anyway? Don't you want her to get better?"

A muscle flexed in his jaw, then he looked up toward a window on the second floor of the house that Carter guessed was Gillian's bedroom.

"Come on," Herman directed, heading away from the house.

Carter followed him, curious to find out why Herman was so upset. They walked down the driveway toward Carter's car. Herman's steps were long and forceful, as if he could barely contain himself.

When they reached the car, the man took a deep breath, his hands curled into fists. "You just met Gillian. This is really none of your business."

"I've decided to make it my business. I care about her."

"If you really care, then you'll convince her to leave the past alone. Some secrets should stay buried."

His words pained Carter because they reinforced the possibility that the candle Gillian had lit that night had started the blaze. "Gillian told me the cause of the fire was reported as undetermined. Is that true?"

Herman didn't say anything for a long moment. "I made sure it was reported that way by the media and that she never saw the official report."

Carter stared at him. "Why?"

"Because the truth could destroy her."

* * *

Carter walked into his hotel room and threw his medical bag on the king-size bed. Herman had refused to elaborate on the cause of the fire, even when Carter had pushed him for the answer.

That worried him.

So did Gillian. He no longer wondered why she had pulled away from him last night. Considering the emotional turmoil in her life, he was just one more complication that she didn't need. Only he wasn't ready to walk away. Or to be pushed out of her life, as Herman seemed determined to do.

He walked over to the sink and splashed some cold water on his face, then grabbed a towel to wipe it off. His day had started early at the track, since he'd wanted to make time for the trip out to Robards Farm.

Carter still needed to go back to Del Mar this evening and double-check a couple of the horses scheduled to race tomorrow. It was difficult to keep his mind on his work when he kept thinking about Gillian. He could still smell the sweet scent of her perfume on him. It clung to his clothes and invaded his senses.

At least he'd see her again on Monday. It seemed like too long, but after the way Herman had acted he was fairly certain he wouldn't be welcome back at the ranch anytime soon. Of course, he could still call her, just to make sure she was all right.

He tossed aside the towel, then walked over to the bed to retrieve his cell phone from the bag. Just as he started to dial the Robards phone number, a knock sounded at the door.

Surprised, he ended the call, hoping there wasn't trouble with any of the horses at the track. Hoping even more that he'd find Gillian standing on the other side of the door.

When he opened it, his disappointment was quickly overcome by the shock of finding his little brother standing in the hallway.

"Hey, Carter," Noah greeted him. "What's going on?"

Noah Phillips wasn't so little anymore, standing almost the same height as Carter. At twenty-one, he was just starting to fill out his lanky teenage body and had the same mischievous gleam in his blue eyes that used to signal imminent trouble.

"What are you doing here?" Carter asked in astonishment.

Noah peered inside the hotel room. "Are you going to invite me in? Or do you have company?"

"Come in," Carter said, pulling his brother into a bear hug. He noticed Noah had deflected the question about his sudden appearance in San Diego. That was just another clue that something was up.

"It's good to see you again, Carter." Noah patted his shoulder, then stepped away from his brother and looked around the hotel suite. "Nice room."

"How are Mom and Dad?" Carter said, still puzzled by Noah's sudden arrival. "Is everything all right at home."

"Everything's fine," Noah assured him. He dropped, his duffel bag onto the floor. "Do you mind if I camp out here for a couple of days?"

Carter closed the door. "Aren't you supposed to be moving back to college this week?"

"Well, here's the deal," Noah said, turning around to face him. "I've decided that I'm not going back to college. That's what I wanted to talk to you about when I called the other night."

Carter stared at him. "I hope you're joking."

"The only joke about college is my grades. Have you seen them?"

"Mom told me you've been struggling."

"That's because I want to take pictures. It's all I've ever wanted to do."

Carter walked over to the mini refrigerator and pulled out two beers. "Want a soda?"

"I'll take a beer. I'm legal now, you know."

Carter knew his brother might be old enough to drink, but he wasn't mature enough to make a life-altering decision like dropping out of college. And yet, Noah and Gillian were almost the same age. It made Carter feel old and he wondered again at the wisdom of becoming involved with her. Yet, he knew he couldn't walk away.

He pulled two bottles of beer out of the refrigerator, then handed one to Noah before sitting down on the small sofa. "I still don't get why you want to leave college. Aren't you taking a photojournalism class? That should give you plenty of opportunities to take pictures."

Noah sighed as he unscrewed the cap on his bottle. "I've never wanted to take news photographs. I'm more interested in the art and design of photography. The best way to learn about that is to go out and do it."

"We can't always do what we want."

Noah rolled his eyes. "I know. You've told me that at least a thousand times. So let me ask you a question, Carter. Why can't we?"

Carter took a deep swig of his beer. They were so different that sometimes he wondered how they could be related. Noah had always been the impulsive one in the family. Maybe it was because Carter had always been the one to pick up the slack.

"Life comes with responsibilities," he said, wincing at how heavy and dull the words sounded to his own ears. "How will you support yourself if you quit college?"

"I'll find a way," Noah said. "That's part of the adventure."

"Can't you at least wait until you graduate? You know I'm willing to pay the rest of your way."

Noah walked over to the sofa and sat down beside his brother. "Hey, you smell good. Have you started wearing perfume?"

"It's not mine."

Noah grinned. "Even better. So who is she?"

"Stop trying to change the subject," Carter said. "We're talking about you."

But Noah had never been one to follow directions. "Mom will be happy to know you're seeing someone.

She's worried you won't ever find Miss Right. Of course, she worries about you all the time."

Carter found that difficult to understand. His mother had a chronic illness but spent time worrying about him? He made plenty of money and made sure all their needs were met. The last thing he wanted was to cause her any worry or distress.

"So will I get to meet her while I'm here?" Noah asked him.

Carter hesitated. "She has a horse racing at Del Mar next Sunday, but it sounds like you'll be leaving before then. Are you really serious about this?"

"Yeah, I'm serious." Noah tipped up his beer. "So why can't I meet her before I leave?"

"Look, we're just friends," Carter said, growing irritated with the conversation. He didn't understand his relationship with Gillian well enough himself to explain it to his brother.

Noah arched a brow. "Well, you two must be pretty close friends to have that much of her perfume on you."

"So what's your plan?" Carter asked him. "Are you just going to roam the country looking for great shots?"

Noah flashed a grin. "Sounds great, doesn't it? Actually, I'm headed for China at the end of the week. A photographer whose work I admire hired me as his assistant. It's the best way to learn the craft."

"China?" Carter was still trying to grasp the fact that Noah was giving up on college.

"That's right. I'm flying out of San Francisco and

thought this would be a good time to see you before I left."

Carter took another swig of his beer. "Are you sure you don't want to rethink this? What if something happens to me? How would you make enough money to take care of Mom and Dad without a college education?"

Noah looked perplexed by his big brother's reasoning. "I don't want to live in a what-if world, Carter. I want to live for today."

Carter understood and even envied Noah for that luxury.

"Besides, Mom and Dad were the ones who encouraged me to do this."

He didn't want to argue with Noah anymore, especially since it was obvious he wasn't going to change his mind. "How about another beer?"

"Sounds good. Now tell me the truth about your woman. Is it serious or not?"

He grabbed two more bottles from the refrigerator. "Well, first of all, she's not my woman. We've only been out on one date."

Noah leaned back on his elbows. "So tell me what she's like?"

Carter considered how best to describe Gillian, picturing her in his mind. "Well, she's a great artist. I bought one of her paintings. She's beautiful, smart, sexy and fun."

"But just more of a friend, right?"

Carter heard the sarcasm in his voice and realized his brother was even smarter than he thought. "The problem is she's only twenty-two."

Noah stared at him. "So?"

"So that's much too young for me," Carter replied, wondering why it wasn't as obvious to his brother as it was to him. "She's just starting her life and deserves some fun and excitement."

"That's true," Noah said, taking a deep swig of his beer. "Maybe *I* should hook up with her instead of you."

Jealousy, hot and swift, rose up inside of him. "Over my dead body."

Noah laughed. "That's more like it. Hell, Carter, if you're hot for the woman, just go for it. Don't let age or anything else stop you." Noah looked at his brother. "You deserve some happiness, too."

Carter pondered his words as he took another swig of his beer. "I'll only be in California for a couple more weeks. That doesn't leave much time for anything besides friendship."

"You've never heard of e-mail and the Internet? Phone sex? Frequent flier miles?" Noah grinned. "When there's a will, there's a way if you really want a relationship."

His brother was right. Carter did want to be more than a friend to Gillian. The only question now was what she wanted.

Twelve

Carter almost made it out the door of the stable at Del Mar when he saw trouble headed toward him. Robbie Preston led a two-year-old stallion named Kiss For Luck and the expression on the trainer's face told Carter he wasn't going to make it to his appointment at the Arcano Gallery on time.

"We've got a problem," Robbie announced.

Carter saw the reason as soon as he looked at the horse. Blood smeared his nostrils, an indicator that the horse might be suffering from EIPH, also known as Exercise-Induced Pulmonary Hemorrhage. It was a condition serious enough to make a horse ineligible to race for a minimum of ten days. Kiss For Luck was scheduled to race tomorrow and was one of Quest Stables' most promising horses.

"Let's get him back to his stall," Carter said, turning around to head back into the stable.

The races had already begun this afternoon and throngs of people filled the stadium and milled about the grounds. He could hear the announcer's blare over the speaker system and the periodic roar of the crowd as they cheered on their favorite horse.

He needed to let Gillian know that he was going to be late, so he grabbed his cell phone, then dialed directory assistance for the number to the art gallery.

"City, please?" the operator asked.

"San Diego," he said, watching the horse ahead of him for any signs of distress. "I need the number for the Arcano Gallery."

A moment later, an automated voice recited the number. Carter punched it into his cell phone, then hit the send button. The call was picked up on the first ring, but had gone directly to voice mail.

"Hello," said a pleasant female voice. "You've reached the Arcano Gallery. If you'd like to leave a message, please dial one now."

He swallowed a groan of frustration as he hit the right button, then waited for the beep. "My name is Dr. Carter Phillips," he began, "and Gillian Cameron is expecting me to bring one of her horse portraits to the gallery this afternoon. Please tell her I'm still at the racetrack at Del Mar and I'm not sure how long I'll be here. If she wants to reach me, my cell phone number is 859-555-1414."

Carter ended the call and stuck the phone back in his pocket, wishing he and Gillian had exchanged cell numbers. If she didn't get the message, she might think he'd stood her up. He knew how important this gallery showing was to her and didn't want to disappoint her.

Robbie led Kiss For Luck into his stall while Carter retrieved his medical bag. EIPH was caused by bleeding in the lungs after strenuous exercise or sudden exertion. Thoroughbreds were especially susceptible to it and it often occurred with no external signs.

Melanie approached them, still wearing her jockey silks from an earlier race. She'd been riding Sir Lancelot's Lady and had finished fourth, not a bad showing for the filly's maiden race. "How is Kiss For Luck? Will he be able to run tomorrow?"

"I don't know yet," Carter said, pulling out a case that contained a flexible fiber-optic endoscope from his bag. "I need to check her airways for blood."

Melanie turned to her brother. "Marcus said he'd cool down Sir Lancelot's Lady. He wants you to stay here with Kiss For Luck, then give him a full report."

Robbie gave a brisk nod and started to say something, then shook his head. Carter knew the youngest Preston didn't like taking orders from Marcus, but at least the two men seemed willing to try to make it work for the sake of Quest Stables. He'd even seen them having a civil conversation earlier in the day.

Carter pulled on some latex gloves, then picked a syringe and filled it with a mild sedative. Robbie still held the horse's lead, murmuring softly to the stallion to calm him down.

Despite his quick-fire temper, Robbie did have a way with horses. Carter waited until the horse had stopped moving around so much in the stall, then injected him in the flank area.

"We'll have to wait a few minutes for it to take effect." Carter used that time to set up the equipment for the endoscopy, including a small television monitor that would broadcast the images from the tiny camera attached to the endoscope.

Melanie leaned against one wall of the stall. "What else can go wrong for Quest? It seems like our bad luck is never going to end."

"We can't give up," Robbie said. "We'll get back in the game. We just have to find a way to prove the true lineage of Leopold's Legacy."

Melanie looked at Carter. "Any progress in that area yet?"

He shook his head. "I'm still working on it."

Robbie's brow furrowed. "What are you two talking about?"

Carter turned to him, aware that Robbie wouldn't let it go until he knew what was happening. "Picture of Perfection might have the same sire as Leopold's Legacy. They look almost identical and Apollo's Ice is listed as the stud, just like he was for Leopold's Legacy."

Robbie's eyes widened. "Why didn't anyone tell me? This might be the break we've been waiting for!"

"We didn't tell you because the owner of the horse refuses to let us take a blood sample," Melanie explained. "You can hardly blame her, given the scrutiny we've had to endure. If word got out that there was doubt about Picture of Perfection's lineage, she'd be facing the same kind of scandal. The track officials here might even scratch her horse from the Pacific Classic."

Robbie nodded. "I see the problem. But if there's a question about Picture of Perfection's lineage, then it's the owner's responsibility to have him tested. We could tell her firsthand about what happens if those suspicions get leaked…."

"That sounds too much like blackmail," Melanie said. "We're not that desperate yet, are we?"

Robbie turned on his sister. "I'd never blackmail her. I wouldn't wish what we've been going through on our worst enemy. But Quest is going to be *banned* from racing horses in North America if we don't resolve this issue. If I can just talk to her…"

"No," Carter interjected. "I'm handling it."

Robbie looked at him in surprise. "You know her?"

"He's dating her," Melanie told her brother. "I know Carter wants to find the answer as much as we do."

"Good." Robbie looked at Carter. "Just do whatever you can to convince her to do the DNA test. And if you need help, let me know."

Carter appreciated the offer, but he didn't intend to take him up on it. Robbie's loyalty was to his family and Quest Stables, as it should be. He didn't even know Gillian or how much she had to lose.

"Kiss For Luck is sedated enough to start the test," Carter said, ready to change the subject. He walked into the stall and moved to the front of the horse. Pulling on another pair of latex gloves, he examined the nostril area of the horse first, gently wiping away the smeared blood with a cotton swab.

"Well?" Melanie asked. "What do you think?"

"It looks like it might just be a scrape," Carter replied. "But we'd better be sure. If one of the track officials noticed the blood, they'd insist on an internal exam before allowing him to race.

Picking up the endoscope, he directed Robbie to hold the horse's head steady. Then he gently inserted the flexible tube into one nostril. The instrument was an excellent tool to observe the airway of a horse, including the larynx, sinuses, guttural pouches and trachea. As he performed the examination, Carter watched the television monitor for any signs of bleeding.

"What do you see?" Robbie asked, staring at the screen.

"It looks clear to me," Carter replied. "I don't see any blood."

Melanie breathed a sigh of relief. "So it is just a scrape. That means Kiss For Luck can race tomorrow."

"That's right." Carter gently removed the endoscope

from the horse, then cleaned it off with disinfectant. When he was finished, he began packing up the rest of his equipment.

His cell phone rang and Carter picked it up. "Hello?"

"Carter, this is Andrew."

Carter bit back a sigh of frustration as he recognized the voice of the oldest Preston sibling, Quest's business manager. A quick glance at his watch told him he was already an hour late for his meeting with Gillian at the gallery. "Hey, Andrew. How are you?"

"Fine," he said. "I just wanted to check in with you to see how things are going at Del Mar. Are all the horses healthy?"

"They're good." Carter told him about the medical status of each of the horses and the endoscopy he'd just performed on Kiss For Luck. He'd been reporting to Andrew periodically since arriving in California, but realized now that he hadn't updated him in a while.

"I'm glad to hear you're on top of things out there," Andrew told him. "I've been keeping in touch with Marcus, too, but it's nice to have his reports confirmed."

"How is everything back in Kentucky?" Carter asked him.

Silence stretched over the line, then Andrew said, "As well as can be expected, I guess. I've been negotiating with several of my contacts at the International Thoroughbred Racing Federation. I want to make certain that Quest horses can continue racing internationally after the North American ban takes effect."

"So you think the ban's really going to happen?" Carter said, feeling sick at the prospect.

"I don't know how to stop it." Andrew heaved a sigh of exasperation. "Brent's been working on it, but we're no closer to figuring out what happened with Leopold's Legacy. Are you?"

"I'm working on it, too," Carter said, hedging around a direct answer. He sensed that if Andrew knew about the possible connection between Leopold's Legacy and Picture of Perfection, he'd want to follow the same aggressive course of action as Robbie.

Carter couldn't let that happen. He had to find a way to convince Gillian to let him take a blood sample before the situation got out of hand.

"I need to go," he told Andrew. "I'll be in touch with you soon."

"All right. Let me know if you need anything out there."

"Will do."

He slid the cell phone into his pocket, then checked on Kiss For Luck. The stallion was coming out of sedation and didn't appear to be suffering any ill effects for it.

"I've got to leave for a while," Carter told Robbie. "Can you keep an eye on the horse for me?"

"No problem. I hope you're on your way to get that blood sample. We don't have time to waste anymore. We need answers now.

"I'll do my best," Carter promised him.

* * *

Gillian walked into the Arcano Gallery, excitement pulsing through her. The art gallery was located in an old warehouse that had been renovated in downtown San Diego. The original brick walls had been fully restored and the copper ceiling stretched high above her. The foundation wall had been upgraded, as well, though small, inconsequential cracks had been left to add character to the building.

She had dreamed of this day for so long. That was just one of the reasons Gillian was determined to ignore her fear that she'd started the fire. Now that she'd had time to think about it, she realized Carter had been right. The fire department would not have missed the fact that a candle started the blaze if it had happened that way.

The hypnotist had told her not to read too much into their first session, because she needed to be able to put it into context. Gillian kept telling herself to just be patient and wait until all her memories had been restored before trying to determine what had really happened that night.

For now, she was going to concentrate on the present. In just five days, the Arcano Gallery would be displaying her artwork for the public to see. It was a huge first step in establishing herself in the California artists community. If that wasn't exciting enough, Picture of Perfection was racing in the Pacific Classic two days after the opening.

All her dreams were finally coming true.

Gillian looked around the large gallery. It was empty, though she could hear faint strains of jazz emanating from the back room. Checking her watch, she noticed she was a little early for their two o'clock appointment and decided to use the extra time to peruse the Arcano exhibits currently on display.

She found the art in the gallery as unusual as the owner himself. Jon Castello didn't limit himself to a certain style of painting—he embraced anything that resonated with him. They'd had a fascinating discussion about it at the symposium she'd attended in San Francisco over spring break.

His latest work was featured on the front wall of the gallery. It was a series of five paintings called *The Cavern* and depicted the same beach cavern from several different angles. A play of light gave an ethereal quality to the otherwise dark and brooding portraits. Gillian studied the paintings for several minutes before she realized the artist was in the room with her.

He was a short man with a stocky build and an unruly mop of thick gray hair. Pale blue eyes studied her from behind a pair of thick, black-rimmed glasses. The oversize white shirt he wore was covered with paint and he was holding a small brush in his hand.

"I'm sorry, Mr. Castello," she said, turning around to face him. "I didn't see you there."

"I've asked you before to call me Jon. We don't stand on ceremony here."

"All right," she said with a smile. "Jon."

He pulled a dirty hand towel out of his back pocket and started wiping the wet brush with it. "I'm thrilled my work has held your concentration for so long. Do you like it?"

She hesitated. "It's interesting. You're very talented."

"Yes, yes," he said, dismissing her compliment with a wave of his hand, "but tell me how the paintings make you feel?"

She turned back to study the series. "Your use of light is very inventive, but I find the overall effect quite disturbing."

He moved to stand beside her. "Perfect! Then I accomplished my goal."

She was relieved her critique didn't offend him. "It's very different from my work. To tell you the truth, I was somewhat surprised you invited me to do a showing at your gallery."

"There's a raw energy in your horse portraits that I believe will appeal to many of my patrons."

Now that the gallery showing was almost upon her, Gillian was getting a little nervous. "You don't think it will be too…one-dimensional? All of my portraits are of horses."

He shook his head. "As long as a subject engages your heart, soul and mind, I see no reason to change it. A true artist always has doubts about his work and strives to perfect it. That's what I did with this cavern series until I lost my interest in it. Now I have a new subject that is absorbing all my attention."

Jon made it sound so simple. Gillian told herself to relax and just enjoy the ride. Even if the critics hated her work, she'd learn something from the experience.

"Do you work here?" she asked, looking at the paint stains on his shirt and hands.

"Sometimes." He examined the dark stains in the crevices of his fingernails, as if he couldn't figure out how paint had gotten there. "I find it inspiring to be surrounded by my previous work. It's quiet here, too, since I don't have to deal with nosy neighbors or children making a racket at all hours of the day and night. I simply come here, turn off the telephone and paint."

"It sounds wonderful."

"You're welcome to use my studio anytime you wish, day or night. It's in the back of the gallery and I usually open it to my interns and a few select acquaintances."

Gillian was flattered by the invitation. "Thank you. I'm between projects at the moment, but I may take you up on that offer sometime soon."

His brow crinkled. "Between projects? How is that possible? An artist is always working, my dear Gillian, even if it is only in his or her own mind."

Gillian wondered if she'd ever come close to matching his intensity level. It was obvious that Jon Castello lived and breathed his work. It was part of him, as if paint ran through his veins instead of blood.

"Did you bring the portrait?" he asked, sticking both the brush and towel back in his pocket.

She checked her watch, surprised to find it was now well after two o'clock. Carter had told her that he'd be here by now, but there was no sign of him.

"The man who bought it promised to bring it here today. I expect him at any moment."

"That's right," Jon said, wrinkling his crooked nose. "You sold your best work to the highest bidder, didn't you?"

"The money went to charity," she reminded him, aware that the economic side of their craft was distasteful to some artists. Gillian wasn't one of them. She saw no virtue in being a starving artist. Still, she didn't value her work according to how much money it earned her, but rather how much pleasure she got from it.

"We can take your photograph while we wait for him," Jon said, walking over to the reception desk.

"My photograph?"

"For the main press release. Another necessary evil, I'm afraid, but publicity does help to draw a crowd."

She remembered Shirley Biden commenting on an ad she'd seen in the newspaper. "Hasn't that already been done?"

He smiled. "Oh, I've been dropping little tidbits about your exhibit here and there, mainly to some friendly art critics. This photo will be for a full-blown ad to really draw the patrons into the gallery."

He picked up a digital camera from the desk, then glanced over at the answering machine. "Looks like I've got a message."

A moment later, Gillian heard a familiar voice. "It's Carter," she said, listening to his message.

Jon wrote down the phone number using neat, block print, then handed it to her. "Please encourage him to bring the portrait here as soon as possible. I want to get the collection up on the walls by Thursday. If I'm not around, my intern Amy will be."

"I'll make sure it gets here," she promised, reaching for her cell phone. But when she dialed Carter's number, it went straight to voice mail.

"Looks like we're playing phone tag today," she said, then began to leave a message for him. "I'm just leaving the gallery, Carter, so I'll meet you at your hotel and pick up the portrait there. See you soon."

Jon frowned at her as she ended the call. "Is it really necessary for you to go to this man's hotel room?"

His reaction unnerved her. Jon had never even met Carter, but his dislike was palpable. Perhaps he thought Carter had changed his mind about lending her the painting, but Gillian wasn't too worried. Carter had given her his permission to use it, and she believed he was a man of his word.

At least, she wanted to believe that.

"He hasn't changed his mind," she assured him. "I can drop off the portrait tomorrow, if that works for you. Or even tonight."

"Tomorrow will be fine." He said briskly, "I'll be out of town for the day, but as I said before, Amy will be here." Jon held up the camera. "Now all we need is your picture and we're set."

"Let me fix my hair first," Gillian said.

"No, no, no," Jon cried. "I want you to look natural, my dear Gillian. To look real."

"I look awful," she began, but he snapped the photograph before she could make a move.

He looked at the display screen at the back of the camera. "Yes, it's quite lovely."

Gillian reached for her purse, not certain she wanted to see the picture. "Is there anything else I should do before Friday?"

Jon set the camera on the desk. "Why don't you stop by on Wednesday, say around three o'clock? That will give us a chance to go over any last-minute details about the showing."

"I'll look forward to it."

As Gillian left the gallery she found herself very eager to see Carter again. That last kiss they'd shared still lingered in the back of her mind and she wondered if she'd been using her nightmares and the other obstacles in her life as an excuse not to get involved.

Maybe if she really let down her guard, she would find an ally in Carter. And a lover. It would be so nice not to have to face all her problems alone, even for just a little while.

Thirteen

Gillian thought she'd gone to the wrong room in the hotel when a lanky young man answered the door.

"Oh, I'm sorry," she began, glancing at the room number on the door.

"You must be Gillian," the man interjected, a curious gleam in his blue eyes. "I'm Noah Phillips, Carter's brother. He told me to expect you."

If she looked hard enough, Gillian thought she could see the resemblance between them, though Noah was younger and had shaggy red hair. They did share the same unusual blue eyes and an identical dimple in their right cheek.

The biggest difference between them was that Noah

still had a boyish air about him that made him seem much younger and more carefree than his older brother.

"Come on in," he said, holding the door open for her. "Carter's still at the track in Del Mar, but he should be back soon."

She walked inside the hotel room, disappointed that Carter wasn't here. "I just came by to pick up the horse portrait, then I'll be on my way."

Noah grinned. "I've received very firm instructions not to let you go until Carter gets back. You don't mind if I hold you hostage, do you?"

His smile was contagious and she found herself grinning back at him. "It depends. Do you have anything good to drink?"

"Absolutely." He walked over to the mini refrigerator situated in the corner of the room. "We've got soda, both diet and regular, beer, bottled spring water and premium orange juice. Only the very best brands for such a beautiful captive."

Gillian's cheeks warmed. "I'll have a diet soda, please."

He retrieved two sodas from the refrigerator, then handed one to her as they both sat down at the small table.

"Don't worry," Noah said. "I'm not hitting on you. Beautiful was one of the words Carter used to describe you, as well as smart, fun and sexy."

Her blush deepened. "Oh?"

"My brother would kill me if he knew I told you,

but that's what makes it all the more fun. I hope you don't mind."

She took a sip of her soda, not quite sure what to make of Carter's younger brother. He certainly wasn't as reserved as his big brother, or as serious.

Concern darkened Noah's blue eyes. "If you do mind, I apologize. I wasn't trying to offend you."

"Oh, I'm not offended at all. You're just a lot different than your brother.

His grin returned. "I'm the comic relief in our family. Carter's the responsible one. The perfect son. So naturally, I have to be just the opposite."

"How long have you been in San Diego?"

"I got here yesterday and I'm headed for San Fracisco tomorrow and then China, so I wanted a chance to surprise Carter before I left."

Now Gillian understood why Carter hadn't mentioned his brother's visit to her. She wondered how the two of them got along and why Noah had referred to Carter as the perfect son. Despite his jovial tone, there had been a strange undercurrent to his words.

She realized that despite her attraction to Carter, she really didn't know much about him. That's what made it all the more bewildering that she felt so safe with him. She'd been attracted to men before, but he was different. The fact that he'd witnessed her hypnotherapy session had given him a glimpse into her life that no one had ever seen before.

"How's the soda?" Noah asked.

"Fine." She took another sip, then set it on the table. "So what will you be doing in China?"

His face lit up at the question. "Taking a lot of pictures."

"You're a photographer?"

"I hope to be someday. I'm traveling as a photographer's assistant and he tells me we're going to see places where most tourists never go."

"Sounds like a great trip."

Noah looked thoughtful. "Yeah, I think so, too. It's always been my dream to travel around the world. I wish Carter would follow his dream…"

Before he could continue, the door opened and Carter walked inside. His gaze went straight to Gillian and she felt a strange twisting in her chest as she rose to her feet. "Hello, Carter."

"Hello, Gillian." He closed the door behind him, then set his medical bag on a chair. "I see you've met my brother."

"I've been telling her you're a con man who preys on beautiful women," Noah said, "but I don't think she believes me. I should have brought the mug shots to back up my story."

Carter scowled at him. "Don't you have to pack or something?"

Noah grinned as he rose out of the chair. "No, but I'll go take a shower so the two of you can have some time alone."

Carter waited until Noah disappeared into the

bathroom, then turned to Gillian. "In case you hadn't noticed, my brother thinks he's a comedian."

"I noticed," Gillian replied. "He is very funny."

"Don't encourage him," Carter warned with a shake of his head. He walked over to the closet to retrieve the painting. It was neatly wrapped in brown paper and tied with a piece of string.

"Here's the portrait. I'm sorry I didn't meet you at the gallery today. One of the Quest horses had a medical problem and I had to check it out."

"I understand."

As he handed her the painting, their fingers touched, but neither one of them broke the contact.

"How have you been?" Carter asked her. "I've been worried about you."

"I'm fine," she assured him. The last time he'd seen her had been right after her therapy session, when she'd been shaken by the very real possibility that she might have started the fire.

"I have another appointment with Christina tomorrow afternoon," Gillian said.

"Can I be there?" he asked, surprising her with the request.

She thought about it for a moment, then nodded. It had been nice to have someone to confide in after the last session. Besides, he might hear her say something that would help her understand the events of that night.

"Are you sure?" Carter asked her. "I don't want to intrude."

"I want you there." *I want you.* The unspoken words were on the tip of her tongue, and if his brother hadn't been in the bathroom, she might have said them out loud. Instead, she pulled the portrait from his hands and took a step back.

Carter walked her to the door. "I'll see you tomorrow, then."

"Three o'clock," she informed him.

He leaned close to her, and for a moment, Gillian thought he was going to kiss her. Then Carter pulled back, a muscle twitching in his jaw. "Let me carry that downstairs for you."

The bathroom door opened and Noah stuck his freshly washed head out. "How can I eavesdrop on you two if you leave?"

Gillian smiled in spite of herself. "Goodbye, Noah. It was nice meeting you. Have a great trip."

"Thanks, Gillian. Don't let my brother's tough guy act fool you. He's crazy about you."

Carter escorted her out the door. "Let's go."

He walked with her to the parking lot and carefully loaded the portrait into the backseat of her car. "Sorry about Noah. He's always taken great pleasure in trying to embarrass me."

"I think you're lucky to have a brother," she said wistfully. "I wish I had one. Or a sister."

"I used to try to sell him when he was little, but no one would take me up on the offer. Believe it or not, he was even more obnoxious then."

That made her laugh and it was easy to see the love Carter had for Noah, despite his exasperation. She opened the driver's door. "Well, if Picture of Perfection wins the Pacific Classic on Sunday, I might take you up on that offer."

"Don't tempt me," he said, giving her a long look before backing away from the car.

Gillian drove away, feeling oddly energized. Something told her that Noah hadn't been joking about Carter's feelings for her. She hoped it was true, because she was starting to fall in love with the man herself.

Carter arrived at Robards Farm a little before three o'clock the next day.

Gillian met him at the door with a nervous smile. "I'm glad you made it," she said. "Christina's earlier appointment canceled so she's here and ready to get started."

He reached out to touch her arm. "Are you sure you're ready for this?"

She took a deep breath, then nodded. "I think I can handle it."

Carter hoped she was right. His conversation with Herman and the man's adamant refusal to divulge the cause of the blaze concerned him. If that candle had been the cause of the fire, he wasn't sure Gillian would ever be able to forgive herself.

Gillian led him into the living room where Christina was already seated in a chair. He greeted her, then took a wing chair opposite hers.

"Not there," Christina said, as soon as he'd taken his seat. "I'd like you to sit on the sofa this time, Carter, and for Gillian to sit there. That will make her less likely to fall asleep like she did last time."

Carter traded places with Gillian, aware of the concern clouding her eyes. Falling asleep during the last session had prevented her from recovering any more memories from the fire. Now she wouldn't have that refuge.

Christina gave her a gentle smile. "We're going to delve a little deeper this time, so I think it's important that we not have any unexpected interruptions. Is your godfather home or are you expecting him or anyone else to arrive soon?"

"No, I'm not expecting anyone," Gillian replied. "Herman's attending a funeral for a friend of his out of town. He won't be home until tomorrow or the next day."

"All right, then let's begin."

Carter leaned back against the sofa, watching Gillian. Noah might have a big mouth, but he'd been right about one thing. Carter was crazy about her.

It left him in a difficult position. Melanie and Robbie knew that Picture of Perfection might hold the key to resolving the Leopold's Legacy scandal. If Apollo's Ice *wasn't* Picture of Perfection's sire, either, then they might be able to put together a DNA profile between the two horses that would reveal the identity of the real sire.

If that sire was an unregistered pedigreed horse, the

owners of the horse would have to officially document the evidence, then present it to the Jockey Association to register the sire as a Thoroughbred. That would mean Picture of Perfection and Leopold's Legacy would be considered true Thoroughbreds, qualified to race in North America. They'd also be qualified to race if their sire was a Thoroughbred registered internationally. If the mystery sire wasn't a Thoroughbred, then it was over—for both of them.

So where did that leave him? Torn between his feelings for Gillian and the loyalty he owed to Quest Stables. A damn difficult place to be.

"I'd like you to close your eyes," Christina directed Gillian, "and take ten long, slow deep breaths."

Gillian's eyes fluttered shut as she followed Christina's instructions. He could see her hands clenched on the arms of the chair and knew she was afraid of what she might remember next.

After Gillian was through taking the deep breaths, the hypnotist continued to ease her into a trance-like state.

"Very good," Christina told Gillian. "With each breath you take, you're feeling more and more relaxed."

Carter watched Gillian as the tiny lines of tension left her face, smoothing the skin near her eyes and mouth. Making her even more beautiful than she was before.

"Now I want you to see yourself at the top of a very long staircase," Christina continued. "I want you to walk down that staircase very slowly, one step at a time. With each step, you'll feel more relaxed."

As he watched them, Carter wondered if he'd be able to undergo hypnosis or if his personality would prevent him from giving that much control over to someone else. He admired Gillian for having the guts to do it, especially when she had no idea what the outcome would be.

"When you reach the landing," Christina continued, "you will be so relaxed that you'll feel like you could float to the top of the ceiling."

Gillian's eyes were still closed, but she didn't seem to be with them in the room anymore. She was in some other place. Some other time.

Christina leaned forward. "Gillian, can you still hear me?"

"Yes," she breathed softly.

"I want you to remember the night of the fire. The night you fell asleep in the living room watching that scary movie. Are you there?"

"Yes."

"Tell me what happens after you light the candle and fall asleep."

Gillian gave a small startled gasp. "Someone is lifting me. It's my daddy. He says it's time for bed."

"Does he carry you to bed?" Christina asked her.

"Yes, but I make him stop. We forgot Morris." Her voice changed slightly, becoming that ten-year-old girl again. *"I want Morris, Daddy. He's on the floor."*

"What is your Daddy doing?"

Gillian didn't speak for a long moment, then she said, "He's laying me on the sofa. Then he picks up Morris, blows out the candle and turns off the television. He leaves the blanket and pillow on the floor."

"Is he taking you up the stairs?" Christina asked her.

"Yes." Then Gillian let out a small scream that made Carter jump.

Christina's eyes widened with concern. "What's wrong, Gillian?"

"Daddy, I'm scared," she cried in that same little girl voice. *"I see a man in the window."*

"Who is the man?" Christina asked her, more urgency in her voice now.

Gillian shook her head. "I don't know. Daddy says there's no one there, but I saw him. I know I saw him."

Her words made Carter's skin prickle. If she was right, then someone *had* started that fire on purpose. Yet, why would Herman conceal that information—unless it was someone he wanted to protect?

Carter shook that unsettling thought from his head, certain there had to be another reason. Herman loved Gillian like his own daughter.

"Daddy doesn't believe me," Gillian whispered. Her eyes were open now and staring straight ahead. A lone tear trickled down one cheek.

"Gillian," Christina said gently, "tell me what happens next."

"Daddy carries me to bed. He tucks me and Morris under the covers. I'm still afraid of the man in the window, so after he leaves I pull the covers over my head."

"Do you fall asleep?"

"Yes."

"Then what happens."

Gillian's eyes widen as fear contorts her face. "I smell smoke! It's dark. I have to find the door."

Carter half rose to his feet at the anguish he heard in her voice, but Christina waved him back.

"You're all right, Gillian. I want you to float to the top of the room. You're just watching everything that's happening below you."

But Gillian couldn't hear her. "Where's the door!" She began to cough, her throat constricting as if she truly was suffocating on smoke.

"Gillian," Christina said, her voice louder now. "You're safe here with me and Carter."

"Carter," Gillian said dreamily. Her breathing eased and she stopped coughing.

Christina looked relieved. "There's no more smoke, Gillian. You have a giant bubble around you."

Carter watched as Gillian closed her eyes once more and took a deep, cleansing breath. He felt physically drained and was relieved that the session was almost over. He hated seeing her relive that awful night. At least now they knew that Gillian hadn't started the fire.

"I want you to go down another staircase," Christina

told her. "Only each step of this staircase will take you farther back in your memory, before the fire and before you saw the man in the window. Even before you sneaked downstairs to watch the scary movie. I want you to remember that day."

Carter frowned at her. "What are you doing? I think she's had enough."

Christina raised a finger to her lips, then whispered, "She's in a very deep state of hypnosis, much deeper than last time. We need to retrieve as many memories as possible while we have the opportunity."

He didn't argue with her. Gillian wanted to know the truth about the fire that had killed her parents. If this was the only way to do it, then he was determined to stay and see her through it.

"Where are you?" Christina asked her.

"I'm playing in the tree house."

"What do you see?"

Gillian opened her eyes again. "I see Daddy. He's talking to a man. The man is mad. He's yelling at Daddy."

Carter tensed, wondering if this could be the man she saw in the window.

"Can you see the man's face?" Christina asked her. "Do you know him?"

Gillian squeezed her eyes shut. "I don't want to look."

"You can look at him. You're safe now, Gillian. You're in the bubble. Nothing bad can happen to you there."

Gillian's eyes slowly opened. "I don't want to be alone in the bubble."

The anguish Carter heard in her voice made his heart ache. He looked over at Christina. "I think we should stop."

But the hypnotist ignored him. "You're not alone. Carter is with you."

"Okay." Gillian let out a long, soft sigh. "I can see the man now."

"Do you recognize the man's face."

"Yes. He looks scary when he's mad."

Christina glanced at Carter, then turned back to her patient. "Who is the man, Gillian?"

"It's Herman."

Fourteen

Gillian opened her eyes and found both Carter and Christina looking at her.

"How do you feel?" Christina asked her.

"Numb," she said weakly, "and confused."

Christina's face softened. "You don't have to process everything from the session right away. The memories are beginning to come back to you and that can be disturbing when you don't have the full picture yet."

"I know there was a man looking through the window that night," she whispered, the memory sending a chill through her. She looked at Carter and saw the concern in his eyes. "But it's like his face is a blur."

Christina stood up. "The unknown always frightens us the most. Your subconscious is blocking that memory for some reason. It's a form of self-protection."

Her words only caused Gillian more frustration. She remembered every moment under hypnosis—every awful moment. "I don't want to be protected, I just want to finally know the truth!"

She looked over at Carter, who hadn't said a word. "Do you think Herman…" Gillian couldn't finish the sentence, the very possibility that he might have started the fire too horrible to even contemplate.

"I don't know what to think," Carter replied, looking as uneasy as she felt.

"Let's schedule another session for next Monday," Christina said. "I think you'll need that much time for your mind to adjust to this new information."

Gillian nodded, wishing they could meet sooner. Not that she had time for another session, between preparing for her gallery showing and Picture of Perfection's run in the Pacific Classic. Ian was loading the stallion in the trailer early tomorrow morning to transport him to the racetrack at Del Mar.

Christina walked over to Gillian and took her hand, giving it a gentle squeeze. "You can always call me if we need to meet sooner. I understand what a difficult time this is for you."

"Thank you," Gillian said, her emotions right on the edge of spilling over. "I appreciate it."

Gillian escorted the therapist to the front door and

watched her leave. When Gillian turned around, Carter was standing directly behind her.

The urge to fall into his arms was almost irresistible. She took a step back, determined to stay strong, even though she longed for the sanctuary of his big, strong body.

"Are you all right?"

She gave a shaky nod. "I think so. That was quite a session."

"You don't look all right." His eyes narrowed. "I'm worried about you, Gillian."

She turned around and opened the door, her emotions too raw to risk staying in the house with him alone. Her knees felt shaky and she feared crumpling into a pitiful heap in front of him. "I think I probably need some fresh air."

Carter followed her outside, matching her quick stride. She wanted to run and scream, to rail at the fact that her memories were making Herman the villain in her life. She loved her godfather. He was the closest thing to family she had left.

"I think we should talk about it," Carter told her. "You can't keep it all bottled up inside."

"It's not Herman," she exclaimed, quickening her pace. "He loves me. He would never try to hurt me or my parents like that."

When Carter didn't say anything, she looked at him, his expression sending a chill through her body. "What aren't you telling me?"

He hesitated, then shook his head. "I'm not sure it's my place."

"Please," she implored, coming to a halt on the driveway, "if you know something that will help me figure this all out, you've *got* to tell me."

He studied her for a long moment. "Herman was upset when he learned you were trying to recover your memories of the fire. He told me some secrets should stay buried."

The words twisted like a knife in her gut. "Did he say why?"

Carter shook his head. "No, but he did tell me that he was able to keep the fire department from reporting the official cause of the fire to the media."

The earth shifted beneath her and Gillian fought to keep her balance. "You mean it wasn't...undetermined?"

He met her gaze, reaching one hand out to steady her. "No. It was arson."

A sob rose in her throat, but she fought to hold it back. If she started crying now, she feared she'd never be able to stop. The fire had been started deliberately.

I see a man in the window.

She turned around and started walking again, her mind a jumble of thoughts and feelings. None of it made sense. Her parents hadn't had any enemies, at least none that she'd known about. Then again, she'd only been ten years old at the time, so they likely wouldn't have shared that kind of information with her.

His face looks scary when he's mad.

Those words flashed in her mind as she thought about who might want to hurt her parents. Herman had been upset that day, but surely not angry enough to burn their house down with them in it.

"I think you should talk to Herman," Carter told her.

She shook her head. "How can I ask him if he set fire to my house? If he didn't, he'd be so hurt by the accusation that our relationship would never be the same. And if he did—" she glanced over at Carter "—then I'm not sure I ever want to know."

Gillian knew she didn't sound rational, but she didn't know how else to explain it. Herman was the last link she had left to her past—to her parents. If that link was cut, what would happen to her?

A plume of dust in the distance signaled an approaching vehicle, and for a moment she thought it might be her godfather. She wasn't ready to face him yet, not until she figured out what she was going to do.

Then she recognized Ian's red pickup truck and heaved a sigh of relief.

"Does he usually drive that fast?" Carter asked, both of them watching as Ian turned into the driveway that led to Robards Farm. She knew Ian always got antsy before a race, but she'd never seen him treat his pickup like this before. Every time he hit a rut, it bounced in the air, the tires chewing up and spitting out gravel.

Carter put a protective arm around Gillian as Ian hit

the brakes to make the turn toward the house. His heavy-duty tires spun on the loose gravel and he just missed careening into the ditch. When he got control of the vehicle, he drove up beside Gillian and Carter and leaned his head out the window.

"Boy, am I glad to see you, Doc. Something's wrong with Picture of Perfection."

Carter grabbed his medical bag from his car, then reached for the passenger door of the pickup and held it open for Gillian to climb in. He followed after her, the door swinging wide as Ian stepped on the accelerator before Carter even sat down.

He managed to get the door closed as Ian turned the pickup around.

"What's wrong with my horse?" Gillian asked her trainer.

Ian shrugged his bony shoulders. "I don't have a clue and I can't reach his regular vet. He's been fine and dandy all day, but when I went to muck out his stall this afternoon, he just didn't look right. I tried to call you but there was no answer so I took a chance you were outside and drove over."

"What are his symptoms?" Carter asked, holding on to the armrest with one hand and Gillian with the other. The pickup had no visible seat belts and Ian's erratic driving made him wonder if they'd make it to the stable in one piece.

"He's breathing kind of funny," Ian replied. "And

he's sort of shaking all over, but he doesn't look cold. I've never seen anything like it."

For Ian to admit such a thing worried Carter. The man had worked with horses all his life, and if he'd never witnessed a similar condition, then that meant it was probably serious and difficult to diagnose. A dangerous combination.

"Did anything different happen today?" Carter asked. "Is it possible he ate or drank something that caused his condition?"

"I can't think of a thing." Ian raked one hand over his thinning hair. "I've been with Picture of Perfection since dawn, getting him ready to go to Del Mar tomorrow. We just followed his normal routine."

Carter looked at Gillian, aware that the last thing she needed in her life was more stress. That therapy session had been difficult for her, though she was trying to put up a tough facade. Even now, he could see her struggle to maintain control, her expression so tight and brittle that he was afraid one wrong word or look would shatter her.

That's why he'd been reluctant to tell her about Herman's reaction when he'd learned Gillian was delving into her past. Yet he knew she had a right to know the truth. Those nightmares she'd been having were proof that she hadn't really put the past behind her.

Ian turned onto the road that led to Gillian's land. A white stable appeared as they crested a hill and Carter could feel his pulse racing. He didn't want to think about what would happen if Gillian lost Picture of Perfection. She had so much invested in him, both financially and emotionally.

When the pickup truck finally came to a stop in front of the stable, Carter opened the door and climbed out, then watched Gillian do the same. She led the way into the stable, then emitted a gasp of horror as Picture of Perfection collapsed right in front of them.

Carter raced to the stallion's side, trying to determine the cause of his collapse. He checked the horse's pulse and respiration rate. Both were elevated and erratic.

Gillian stood just inside the stall, her hands clasped together. "Oh, Carter, what's wrong with him?"

"I don't know," he muttered, aware that the horse was declining fast. He reached for his bag and opened it, trying to determine the right treatment.

Ian entered the stable, turning his worn cowboy hat in his hands. "What can I do to help?"

"I'm going to take some blood samples for testing," Carter said, pulling a blood test kit from his bag. "He might have contracted an infection or some other blood-borne disease. Maybe even a rare virus."

Gillian moved near the horse's head as Carter injected the needle into a large vein and extracted enough blood to fill three small test tubes. He capped them, then placed them in the insulated container that came with the test kit.

"I need you to take this kit to the vet school at UC-Davis. A friend of mine works there. His name is Dr. Karl Moyers. Tell him I need these results STAT and don't leave until he gives them to you."

"How long will it take?" Gillian asked.

Carter looked at the struggling stallion, knowing they didn't have much time left. "The soonest the tests can be done is sometime tomorrow morning."

"That's better than nothing," Ian exclaimed, looking ready for action.

Carter pulled out the form that came with the test kit, then patted his pockets in search of a pen.

"Here you go," Ian said, handing him a stubby pencil. Carter could hear Gillian speaking soft, soothing words to the distressed horse as he took the pencil and quickly scribbled his name, hotel address and room number at the top of the form. Then he started checking off several boxes on the long list of possible tests. He wanted the full spectrum since he had no idea what had befallen Picture of Perfection so suddenly.

His hand faltered as he came to the last test on the list.

DNA.

Carter checked it before he had time to consider all the implications. It was possible the horse was suffering from a genetic condition and that made the verification of his lineage all the more important.

But there was something even more critical. Protecting Gillian. Carter had put her at risk by doubting

Picture of Perfection's lineage. Doubts he'd relayed to Melanie and Robbie Preston. He trusted both of them not to hurt Gillian, but one wrong slip from any of them could have devastating consequences for her. Even a suspicion that Apollo's Ice wasn't Picture of Perfection's sire could prevent her horse from running in the Pacific Classic. So she needed to know the truth, one way or the other. A truth that he'd let her handle in her own way. A truth that might tear them apart forever.

Carter tucked the form between two of the test tubes, then sealed the kit and handed it to Ian. "Don't forget, his name is Dr. Moyers. Tell him I sent you."

"I'll stay there until it's done," Ian promised. "No matter how long it takes."

Carter nodded, watching as the old cowboy hurried out the stable door. Then he walked back into the stall and saw that Picture of Perfection looked even worse than he had a few minutes ago.

Gillian gazed up at him, tears welling in her big green eyes. "He's dying, Carter."

His heart contracted as he knelt down beside her. He'd never felt so helpless in his life. As a veterinarian, he'd lost animals before. It was a hard lesson that he'd learned earlier in his career. No matter how much he fought, no matter how much he cared, some of his patients just didn't make it.

"We've got to do something," Gillian pleaded, the tears spilling over onto her cheeks.

Do something. Do anything. Carter peered into his

bag, hoping to find a miracle inside. What he did find was a long shot, but it was better than no shot at all. Grabbing the small bottle, he filled up a sterile syringe with epinephrine, mentally calculating the right amount for the horse's weight.

Then he plunged the needle into Picture of Perfection's flank, making sure it hit the thickest part of the muscle.

"What is that?" Gillian asked him.

"Our last hope," Carter told her, knowing she needed to be prepared for what looked like the inevitable. Picture of Perfection was dying and there was nothing more he could do about it.

They sat there in the stall together, watching as the mighty stallion struggled to breathe. The horse's head lay flat on the straw, his eyes half-closed. Carter knew it would be over soon. His long shot was fading fast.

Then it happened.

A twitch of the tail. A weak snort. A few moments later, Picture of Perfection began to lift his head off the straw.

Gillian grabbed Carter's hand. "What's happening?"

Carter stared at the horse in disbelief. "I think the epinephrine's working."

They watched as the horse slowly struggled to his feet, his breathing steadier now and the shaking starting to diminish. The transformation was startling, but Carter didn't want to get Gillian's hopes up too high, especially when he still didn't know the cause of the horse's collapse.

"He's recovering," Carter announced. "I still need to keep a close eye on him, at least until Ian gets back with the initial test results tomorrow morning. It's possible he could still have a relapse."

"But he looks so much better."

"I know." Carter glanced around the neat stable. "But I think I'll camp out here tonight just to be on the safe side."

"Then I'll join you," she said, tipping up her chin. "I won't be able to sleep a wink anyway after everything that's happened today."

Spending an entire night alone with Gillian without touching her seemed almost impossible. But he couldn't touch her now. Not until he told her about the DNA test he'd just ordered.

And this certainly wasn't the time to tell her, since she'd been through an emotional wringer in just the last couple of hours. First the therapy session that implicated her beloved godfather in the fire that killed her parents, then the collapse of her prize racehorse.

"Carter?" Her brow crinkled as she looked at him. "Do you mind?"

"No," he replied, telling himself he could endure anything to make Gillian happy. "I don't mind."

"Good." A smile lit her face. "The stall opposite this one is clean, so we can camp out there. I'll go grab some pillows and blankets from the cottage and you can throw down a couple of straw bales from the hayloft."

He watched her walk out of the stable, his body

tightening at the way her hips moved in those snug denim jeans. Then he headed up to the hayloft. *Straw. Blankets. Pillows.*

It was going to be a long night.

Fifteen

Gillian sat on a thick bed of clean straw and watched Carter check on Picture of Perfection in the stall across from her. The horse seemed fully recovered, but she was glad Carter was here taking such good care of him. His collapse had happened so suddenly that she feared it could happen again.

She leaned against the thick stack of pillows propped up behind her and found herself wishing Carter would pay that kind of attention to her. He'd been a little distant, literally and figuratively, for the last few hours and she couldn't figure out why. His pillow and blanket were bunched up in the opposite corner of the stall, as far away from her as he could get.

In a way she couldn't blame him for pulling back. She couldn't think of any man who would be interested in a woman who was carrying around so much emotional baggage. She'd tried to keep her feelings in check after the therapy session, but Carter was too intuitive not to know how much the session had shaken her. Even now, she didn't like to think about it.

Carter walked out of Picture of Perfection's stall and peeled off his latex gloves. "All his vital signs are normal."

"That's a good sign, right?"

He nodded as he tossed the gloves into a trash can. "He seems fully recovered, which makes me wonder if his collapse was due to some kind of allergic reaction. That's really the only logical explanation for such a drastic turnaround after the shot of epinephrine."

"What would he be allergic to?"

Carter stood at the end of the stall, his tall, athletic build silhouetted against the moonlight shining through the window. "It could be anything. A bee sting or something he ingested. We may never know the cause."

"You must be tired," she said, wondering how long he was going to stand there.

"No, I'm fine," he assured her. "Are you sure you want to stay out here all night? You've got your gallery exhibit opening in just a couple of days. You could probably use a good night's sleep."

"I'm not leaving this stable until Ian gets back with those test results," she said firmly, wondering how many more times he was going to try to get rid of her.

If Carter knew her better, he'd realize that any attempts to make her change her mind usually had the opposite effect. She could be as stubborn as the most temperamental filly.

A shadow crossed his face, then he gave a brisk nod. "Maybe that would be the best. Then we can go over all the test results together."

She watched him walk into the stall and take a seat in his corner. He was only a few feet away from her, but he seemed much farther. She wondered if something could be bothering him, like his brother's departure for China. Gillian had been so caught up in her own problems that she hadn't thought he might be troubled himself.

"What did Noah mean," she began, "when he said he wished you would follow your dream?"

Carter looked up at her. "You shouldn't take Noah seriously."

"So you don't have any dreams?"

A muscle flicked in his jaw. "I didn't say that. Everybody has dreams. Some people can follow them and others have to give them up when faced with other priorities."

"And I take it you fall into the latter category?"

He reclined against his pillow, one hand propped behind his head. "I guess I do."

"What's your dream, Carter?"

He sighed. "I always wanted to teach veterinary medicine, specifically equine medicine. Don't get me wrong, I love my job at Quest Stables, but there is a lot of travel involved. I've always imagined what it might be like to settle down on a few acres of my own and teach at a university."

She heard the wistfulness in his voice and realized how much he regretted giving up that dream. "What's stopped you?"

He lay on the straw, his gaze fixed on the wooden rafters above him. "When my mother got sick two years ago, I knew that she'd be facing increased medical costs. As a salesman, my father doesn't have very good insurance."

"So you gave up your dream to become a teacher so you could take care of your parents."

He looked over at her. "I knew I couldn't help support them and take the pay cut that would come with a professorship. So I made the only choice possible."

Carter made it sound like anyone in his position would do the same, but she knew that wasn't true. From everything she'd experienced, that kind of family loyalty was in short supply these days. She admired him for it, even as she heard the regret in his voice.

"How do your parents feel about it? Does it bother them that you gave up your dream of teaching?"

He looked at her in surprise. "They don't know anything about it and I intend to keep it that way. I made the mistake of telling Noah after I'd had a few too many beers. That's a mistake I won't make again, but he never lets me forget it."

Gillian stared at him. Carter was handsome and noble and so damn sexy that she wanted to throw herself at him and make them both forget the pain and regret that cast such large shadows over their lives.

She slid down into the straw and bunched a pillow underneath her head. The straw looked almost silver in the moonlight and she felt a lonely weariness steal over her. She was so tired of fighting her feelings. So tired of being alone.

"What are you going to do about Herman?" His voice was so soft that Gillian was tempted to pretend she hadn't heard him. She'd been trying to avoid that question all night.

"I don't know," she said at last. "I don't want to believe it's him, but after what you told me and…"

"And?" he prompted.

She swallowed hard, realizing that she had to be honest about everything, especially with herself. "And I found something in Herman's attic a few years ago that makes me suspect there could be a reason my father and Herman were arguing that day."

"What did you find?"

She licked her lips. "A love letter from my mother to Herman, dated a couple of years before the fire."

The silence stretched between them and Gillian waited for him to say the letter didn't point to Herman's guilt or to an affair between them. Waiting for him to say anything that would ease this ache inside of her.

"Did you ask Herman about it?"

"No," she replied. "His wife, Marie, had just died when I found the letter and he was devastated at losing her. I told myself I'd ask him later, but no time ever seemed right. Eventually, I just stuck the letter back in the attic and made myself forget about it."

Carter turned toward her. "I think you have to ask him."

"I know," she said softly. "I'm just not sure I'm ready to hear the answer. I remember my mother acting strangely in the days before the fire. She was so jumpy and nervous. Sometimes the doorbell would ring and she'd make us both hide until whoever it was went away."

"You think she was hiding from Herman?"

She looked at him. "I don't know. Maybe she had an affair with him and she tried to break it off, but he wouldn't let her. The only way to find out is to ask Herman."

Carter rose up off the straw and for a moment Gillian thought he was going to come to her. Then he shifted and lay back down, his face in the shadows. "You don't have to decide anything tonight, Gillian. Why don't you try to sleep? If something happens with Picture of Perfection, I'll wake you up right away."

Disappointment seeped into her veins, mingling with a sense of loneliness that threatened to overwhelm her. She closed her eyes so Carter wouldn't see the tears welling in them. Then she willed herself to sleep, wanting to forget, for even a little while, how alone she really was.

* * *

Carter watched Gillian sleep. She was bathed in moonlight, her long, silky hair pooled around her supple body. She'd thrown off the blanket long ago, allowing the moonbeams to outline the sweet slope of her breasts, then dip into the valley of her slender waist before cresting the inviting curve of her hips. He wanted to trace that light with his fingers, to feel the warmth of her skin and sink into her soft body.

Carter sucked in a deep breath as the fantasy stretched before him. He'd been watching her for hours, wondering if he'd ever get over her. He wouldn't have any choice if she discovered that he'd requested the DNA test from the lab at UC-Davis.

He closed his eyes, wondering if he'd made a mistake. He'd told himself he was doing it to protect her, but maybe that had just been an excuse. He'd been searching for answers about Leopold's Legacy for the past two months. Answers that would allow him to save Quest Stables and keep his job and reputation intact. A job that he needed to take care of his family.

He wanted to take care of Gillian, too. He loved her. It wasn't a sudden realization, but rather a simple truth that he was surprised he hadn't recognized before now. She filled his heart and soul with a joy that he'd never experienced before. A joy so fragile that he knew losing her would break him into a million pieces.

Yet, that's what he'd risked by ordering that DNA

test. And no matter what his motivation, he feared that she would only see it as a betrayal.

He would find out tomorrow when Ian returned with all the test results. In the meantime, Carter was stuck in purgatory, paying for his sins by not allowing himself to touch her. It was almost four o'clock in the morning and his body wouldn't let him sleep. It pulsed with a primal need that only a woman like Gillian could arouse in him.

She shifted on the straw, a small moan escaping from her lips. They parted slightly and his breath hitched at the reaction his body had to that one small movement. He turned away, unable to torment himself like this any longer.

He closed his eyes, willing sleep to overtake him. The sooner morning came, the sooner his fantasies about Gillian would come to a screeching halt. He stretched out to his full length, then heard a strange sound coming from Gillian's side of the stall.

Carter turned around and saw her half sitting up, her fingers clawing the wall of the wooden stall. Her eyes were only half-open and she had a look of panicked desperation on her face. She was in the midst of one of her nightmares, trying to escape from the smoke and flames once more.

He was by her side in an instant, pulling her into his arms. "Gillian, wake up. You're all right. Wake up."

She cried out, then twisted her arms tightly around his neck. "Help me!"

"Gillian," he said in her ear, running one hand over her hair to soothe her. "Wake up now. You've having a nightmare."

Gillian opened her eyes, disoriented for a moment. She looked around the stall, then at Carter. "What happened?"

"You were having a nightmare."

Now she remembered, although the fear and panic the nightmare usually evoked in her were fading fast in the sanctuary of Carter's arms.

She was fully awake now and sensuously aware of his hard body pressed against her own. She moved in even closer, eager to touch every part of him. The odd tension that had hovered between them before now dissolved into a molten heat that warmed the most sensitive parts of her.

"Are you all right now?" he said huskily, unable to hide the desire she saw burning in his eyes.

"No," she said, before he could pull away. "Not yet."

Then she kissed him, her hands moving under his shirt as she released every inhibition she'd ever had toward the opposite sex. She was tired of playing it safe and losing anyway. All she cared about was this man at this moment in time.

Carter groaned low in his throat as her hands slid over his washboard stomach and splayed over his broad chest. "This isn't a good idea...."

She stopped his words with another kiss as she pulled the shirt apart. It gave her a feeling of power that erased the fear that had gripped her for so long.

Carter's hands cradled her hips, his broad fingers tentatively stroking the skin between her jeans and her T-shirt. She could feel the hard evidence of his arousal pressed against her waist as he rained hot kisses on her face and neck.

She sensed his resistance weakening and gave him no chance to retreat. Pushing him back into the straw, she leaned down to lick a sensual trail from his navel along the waistband of his jeans.

His fingers tangled in her long hair. "Gillian, please don't…stop."

She slid down the length of his body, taking his blue jeans and white boxer shorts with her. Then she used her tongue in an erotic exploration of his naked body before finding her way back to his mouth

A low groan rumbled in his chest as he tugged at her jeans until they were down around her knees. She kicked them off, then straddled him, wearing only a lacy pink thong. In one fluid motion, she stripped off her shirt and bra, pulling them over her head and tossing them aside.

His eyes feasted on her, then his hands, then his mouth. She tipped her head back as his tongue circled each taut nipple.

If this was a dream, she didn't ever want to wake up. His touch healed that small place inside of her that had been an aching void for so long. Yet, it wasn't enough. She wanted all of him.

With his face buried in her chest, she reached back

in search of her jeans, then pulled a small foil square from the pocket. She'd been prepared for this moment since their very first kiss. It had been inevitable, a twist of fate that she was finally ready to greet with open arms and an open heart.

She tore open the package, the noise stilling Carter for a moment. He lay back in the straw, allowing her to roll it onto him with trembling fingers. She took her time, then stroked one hand over him in an intimate caress that made his body arch into the air.

Carter reached out and pulled her on top of him, tearing away the tiny strip of lace fabric that was the only barrier between them. Then he was inside her and Gillian gasped as he stretched and filled her so completely.

"I want to watch you," he gasped, lifting her shoulders so he could see her face. She rose up to a sitting position, bracing her hands against his chest as he drove even deeper inside her. The sensation made her moan aloud as she arched her neck back and closed her eyes.

The rhythm of his body carried her higher and higher on the waves of her desire. Carter's hands slid up and over her legs until his fingers found the sweet juncture between her thighs. He stroked her there, his thumbs gently kneading the most sensitive spot hidden beneath the thicket of tight curls.

"Oh, yes," she cried, moving faster on him now as the tremors of release began to overtake her.

"You're so beautiful," he whispered, then rose up

and rocked deep inside of her as she neared the precipice. The movement sent her completely over the edge and Carter caught her cries with his mouth as she came undone. Beneath the explosive vibrations of her climax she could feel the powerful release of his own.

They fell back into the cushion of straw together, their bodies entangled and their ragged breathing the only sound.

For the first time in her life, Gillian had achieved perfection.

It was better than she'd ever imagined.

Sixteen

Gillian awoke to find herself wrapped in Carter's arms, her head resting on his shoulder. She found comfort in the steady rise and fall of his chest and snuggled in even closer to his warm body as she inhaled the sweet aroma of the fresh straw.

They'd fallen asleep right after making love, their bodies still connected. The few short hours of rest left her feeling more refreshed than she'd felt in a long time.

Carter stirred beneath her but he didn't wake. His right arm was draped protectively over her and a thin blanket covered them both. She glanced over at Picture of Perfection, who stood in the stall across from them with his head near the open window. The stallion looked regal and ready for action, with no sign of a relapse from his strange mystery illness.

Gillian turned her attention back to Carter, sliding her hand lightly over the dark hair on his chest. She rested her palm just above his heart, feeling the strong, rhythmic beat beneath her fingers. After last night, she knew for certain she wanted his heart to belong to her. She wanted every part of him.

The way he'd made love to her last night left no doubt in her mind that they belonged together. She didn't want to think about the logistics of a long-distance relationship, with his job in Kentucky and her life in California. At this moment, all she wanted to do was make love with him again.

She leaned up and kissed his jaw, the thick stubble tickling her lips. His eyes opened, then his mouth curved into a sleepy smile. "Good morning, beautiful."

"You don't have to call me that," she said, snuggling against him.

"Yes," he countered, pulling her against him. "I do."

Her body began to tingle as he reached out to caress her cheek, then he moved his hand lower. The gentleness of his touch made her want more. She leaned up to kiss him when the sound of gravel crunching under tires made them both sit up.

"Ian," Gillian guessed, then confirmed it by looking out the window. "He's coming up the driveway."

Carter sat up on the straw. "Where are my pants?"

"Here," she said, tossing them to him. She scooped up her shirt and bra as the sound of the truck grew closer.

"There's no way those tests could be done already," he muttered as he pulled his jeans up over his boxer shorts.

Gillian searched the straw for her thong. "I can't find my underwear."

"There's no time," Carter announced, holding out her jeans. "He's almost here."

She wiggled into them, sans underwear, then quickly ran her fingers through her tangled hair while Carter buttoned up his shirt. She couldn't help but laugh at their predicament.

Carter didn't join her. Worry etched his brow as he turned to her. "Gillian, we need to talk…"

"I know," she said as the door to the stable opened and Ian walked inside. "Later."

Carter watched her walk out of the stall, afraid later would never come. If Ian had those test results, Gillian would soon realize what he'd done and those incredible moments they'd shared last night would become just another nightmare for her.

As Ian approached them, he frowned down at the jumble of pillows and blankets in the stall. "Looks cozy."

Gillian cleared her throat. "We didn't want to leave Picture of Perfection alone last night, although he's much better this morning. Carter gave him a shot of epinephrine."

"Good call, Doc," Ian replied. "How did you figure it out?"

"Call it a shot of desperation," he replied. "I could see the horse was in respiratory distress and the epinephrine was the only drug I had available that might reverse it. I just got lucky."

Gillian walked over to the trainer. "So what did the tests show?"

"I didn't stick around to wait for them after I talked to Dr. Moyers this morning."

Carter spied a hint of pink lace near his foot and kicked some straw over it. "Why is that?"

Ian tipped up his cowboy hat. "Well, remember when you asked me yesterday if Picture of Perfection had anything different in his routine?"

Carter nodded. "Yes."

Ian walked over to the tack box and pulled out a small bottle. "I treated him with Phenylbutazone for a swollen fetlock. It's one of the few medications approved by the California Horse Racing Board as long as you stop using it twenty-four hours before a race. I didn't think it would be a problem, but that vet at UC-Davis told me that a certain lot number of that brand was tainted and there's been reports of it causing anaphylactic shock in horses. I had a bottle of the stuff with me in the cooler, ready to take to Del Mar, so I was able to give it to the vet."

"And it was from the same bad batch," Carter ventured.

Ian nodded. "That shot could have killed him."

"It almost did," Gillian said, reaching out to pet the horse. "Carter saved his life."

Ian reached out to shake Carter's hand. "I appreciate your quick thinking."

Carter knew he didn't deserve the gratitude of either one of them, not after he'd played fast and loose with the blood sample. At least he'd been given a reprieve, since Ian hadn't waited around for the test results. Now he could tell Gillian the truth about what he'd done in his own time and his own way.

His eyes feasted on her as she talked to Ian. Even with straw sticking out of her hair, she looked perfect to him. His body tightened when he thought of the way they'd made love together last night.

He'd resisted her as long as humanly possible, but when Gillian had begun caressing his body with her tongue, he was completely lost.

Carter still felt slightly disoriented from the experience, as if his entire world had been tilted on its axis. The lack of sleep might have something to do with it, although he knew the real reason was Gillian.

Now that she'd come into his life, he never wanted her to leave it.

Ian turned back to Carter, breaking his reverie. "The vet at UC-Davis said there shouldn't be a problem with Picture of Perfection running in the Pacific Classic if he made it through the night. What do you think?"

Carter saw the hopeful expectation on Gillian's face

as she awaited his answer and he was glad he didn't have to disappoint her. "He should be fully recovered by Sunday, so I don't see a problem with him running. Just make sure you destroy that batch of tainted medicine."

"Already done," Ian said with a hint of disgust in his voice. "I contacted that horse supply company, too, and gave them a piece of my mind. They should have contacted all their customers who had received that batch."

"Yes, they should have," Carter agreed. "That's negligence on their part."

"That's exactly what I told them! I also let them know that they'll be facing a multimillion-dollar lawsuit if anything happens to Picture of Perfection because of it."

Carter nodded his approval. Too many people didn't take animal safety seriously, even some of those who worked in the pet food business and animal pharmaceuticals. He was glad Ian was on top of it, though he intended to report the incident, too.

Ian flashed a smile at Gillian. "Well, I guess your horse and I are on our way to Del Mar. This is a momentous occasion. Care to ride along?"

Gillian looked uncertainly at Carter. "Did you want to talk to me first?"

"It can wait," he replied, knowing how excited she was about entering her horse in the Pacific Classic. The sooner they got Picture of Perfection to the racetrack, the easier his adjustment to the new environment would be.

Gillian turned to Ian. "All right, I'll go with you. Just give me a few minutes to change clothes."

Ian looked at his watch. "Don't take too long. It's better to transport him early in the day while it's still relatively cool."

Gillian motioned for Carter to follow her as she walked toward the door. "I hate to ask you this, but would you mind if I stayed at your hotel for the next couple of days? I'm just not ready to face Herman yet and he's due back this afternoon."

"I'd love it," Carter said honestly. "I'm headed back to the hotel now to shower and change, so I'll instruct the front desk to leave you a key to my room."

She smiled up at him. "Then I'll see you later?"

"Definitely," he promised.

Carter watched her leave, grateful that he'd have plenty of time to explain about the DNA test he'd ordered. Maybe he could find some way to make her understand why he'd thought it was necessary, especially after hearing Robbie's threats of going public with their suspicions.

It was another long shot, but he knew Gillian was worth the risk. They'd made a connection last night and he wasn't about to let anything ruin it.

Gillian realized after Carter had left that she couldn't accompany Ian to Del Mar because she was due to meet with Jon Castello later today at the Arcano Gallery. If she wanted to go to Del Mar, she'd have to drive separ-

ately, since Ian wouldn't want to haul her back to San
Diego during his training time with Picture of Perfection.

She could use the extra time anyway to pack a bag
to take with her to Carter's hotel. A thrill shot through
her that they'd be sharing a bed tonight. She didn't
care whether they slept in a bed or a horse stall as long
as they were together.

After a quick stop at Robards Farm to pack an overnight bag, she headed for Carter's hotel in downtown
San Diego. Her gallery showing was scheduled to open
tomorrow and Picture of Perfection was running in his
biggest race on Sunday.

Her life was a whirlwind, but she felt more grounded
than ever, thanks to Carter.

She pulled into the hotel, handing her car keys to the
valet, but carrying her own bag inside. The well-ap-
pointed lobby had a huge marble sculpture of two stallions engaged in battle. She had spent some time
studying it the first time she'd come to Carter's hotel,
when she'd picked up the horse portrait.

Now as she walked past the sculpture, she promised
herself to invite Lily here for lunch sometime at one of
the hotel restaurants so they could analyze the artist's
technique together.

Gillian smiled to herself as she approached the front
desk, wondering if her friend was still with the ear
doctor. No doubt Lily would be thrilled to know that she

and Carter were an item, although Gillian considered their relationship much more than a fling.

"May I help you?" asked the young female clerk standing behind the polished marble counter.

"My name is Gillian Cameron. One of your guests, Dr. Carter Phillips, arranged for a key card to his room to be left here for me."

"Let me check," said the clerk, tapping a few keys on the computer in front of her. "Yes, he did leave those instructions. I'll activate a card for you."

Gillian only had to wait a moment before the clerk returned with a plastic key card in one hand and a large envelope in the other.

"Here you go," she said, handing the key card to Gillian. "Do you already know his room number?"

"Yes, I've been up there before." She turned to go when the clerk called her back.

"Excuse me, Ms. Cameron, would you mind telling Dr. Phillips that this letter just arrived for him by special courier. I've been trying to call his room but there's no answer."

"He probably already left for Del Mar," Gillian told her, "but I can take it up to his room."

The clerk hesitated. "I suppose that would be all right since you are registered as a guest now." She smiled as she handed over the envelope. "Thank you, Ms. Cameron. I appreciate it."

"You're very welcome."

As Gillian stepped into an empty elevator, she

glanced down at the envelope. It was from the veterinary laboratory at the University of California-Davis and Gillian knew it must contain the results of the lab tests that Carter had ordered for Picture of Perfection.

She pressed the button for the fifth floor, then her gaze moved to the courier slip and she saw a note scribbled at the bottom.

Dr. Phillips,
Here are the test results you ordered. I put a rush on the DNA test so you could get it ASAP. Good luck.
Dr. Moyers

She read the note again as everything inside of her froze. But there was no mistake—it was right there in black and white.

I put a rush on the DNA test.

The doors to the elevator opened and Gillian stepped out, feeling as though she was in the middle of another nightmare. She walked to Carter's hotel room and inserted the key card. The green light blinked on and she pushed the door open.

As Gillian walked inside the room, she could hear the shower running in the bathroom and Carter singing a song she didn't recognize in a loud, off-key voice. It was the voice of a happy man.

A man who had gotten everything he wanted.

Any other time she might have laughed at his boisterous solo, but now she just felt like throwing up. She set her bag down by the door, then walked over to a chair by the window to sit down and wait for him.

She tried to think of another plausible explanation for him to request a DNA test, but her mind was a jumble of thoughts and her emotions were too raw to allow her to think rationally.

At last the door to the bathroom opened and a fog of steam escorted Carter into the room. He wore a blue towel wrapped around his waist and nothing else.

He started when he saw her, then smiled. "Gillian, you're early. This is a nice surprise."

She stood up and walked over to him, unable to speak.

Carter knew something had gone terribly wrong since he'd last seen her this morning.

"What is it?" he asked. "Did something happen to Picture of Perfection?"

"You tell me." She thrust out her arm and he looked down to see the envelope in her hand. "Did you order a DNA test for my horse?"

Carter felt a deep flush creep up his cheeks. Then he looked up at her, panic clawing at him. "I can explain."

"Just tell me the truth," she said in an eerily calm voice that worried him more than if she'd been shouting, "because I have to hear you say it."

Carter realized she already knew the answer. He

wished he had told her sooner, because now she'd never believe that he had intended to be honest with her about it.

"Yes," he said at last. "I ordered the test."

Her face contorted as she spun on her heel and headed toward the door.

"Wait," he called after her, not willing to let it end like this. "You can't just walk out of here without giving me a chance to explain."

She whirled on him. "Explain what? That you've been using me to get your precious test? I get it, Carter. You win. You got exactly what you wanted."

He saw pain clouding her green eyes and hurried to correct any misconception about what had happened between them. "I never intended to sleep with you last night…it just happened."

She stepped back as if he'd slapped her and Carter realized his words had come out all wrong.

"Look, Gillian, you know that's not what I meant. I *wanted* to sleep with you last night, wanted it more than anything, but not because I was trying to deceive you. That DNA test was going to happen one way or the other." He kept talking, hoping to come up with some way to make her understand. "I know it sounds stupid, but I thought if I knew the results of the test before anyone else, I could protect you and…"

"Protect me," she echoed, her eyes bewildered by his claim. "From what? The chance to save Robards Farm and my sanctuary? I thought you *cared* about me,

Carter." Her voice cracked. "I thought I meant something to you."

"You do." He raked a hand through his wet hair. "Look, you caught me off guard. Let me get dressed and we'll sit down together and talk this out."

She slowly shook her head. "I can't do this anymore. I'm tired of secrets and lies."

Before he could reply, she picked up her overnight bag and walked out the door. He started after her, then realized he couldn't chase her through the hotel wearing only a towel.

Carter hurried to the dresser, pulling open drawers and flinging clothes onto the bed as he tried to think of something to say to her. The truth was that he had no good explanation. At least, none that would satisfy her.

He didn't waste time putting on shoes or combing his wet hair, drawing some curious looks as he raced down the hallway. Flinging open the door to the stairwell, he took the concrete steps three at a time all the way down to the main level of the hotel.

But it was too late. By the time he reached the lobby, she was already gone.

Seventeen

Carter saw Picture of Perfection standing in his stall at Del Mar and Ian digging through the tack box near him, but he didn't see Gillian. Disappointment washed over him as he slowed his step. He'd been hoping she'd come here after leaving the hotel.

Ian looked up and waved to him. "You should have seen the way Picture of Perfection went through his paces this afternoon. Nobody would ever guess he'd almost died yesterday."

Carter walked over to the horse, giving him a quick evaluation. His eyes were bright and alert, his breathing steady and clear. "He looks like a winner."

"He sure does," Ian agreed. "I told Gillian that

winning the Pacific Classic will qualify him for the Breeder's Cup. If he can place there, she can practically name her price for his stud fees."

Carter's heart skipped a beat. "You talked to Gillian? Is she still here?"

"I haven't seen her since this morning when she was with you." Ian gave him a quizzical look. "Is there something going on here I should know about?"

Carter could hear the crinkle of the unopened envelope in his pocket, but he wasn't planning to show it to anyone except Gillian. "No, I just need to talk to her."

Ian shrugged. "Have you tried her cell phone?"

"Yes," he replied. *Three times.* "She doesn't answer."

"That doesn't sound like Gillian. Maybe her cell phone battery is low or she forgot to take it with her to the gazebo. She paints there practically every day."

Carter nodded, intending to look there next. "Thanks, Ian. I'm sure I'll find her."

Ian looked up at him. "It's easy to find a woman, Dr. Phillips. The hard part is keeping her."

Carter gave him a brisk nod, fearing he was about to learn that lesson the hard way. He turned around and headed for the stalls of the Quest Stables horses, knowing he couldn't shirk his duty as head veterinarian no matter how much he'd screwed up his life.

He didn't hurry his examination of the six horses, giving each a thorough check before moving on to the next stall. After seeing how upset Gillian had been, he wanted to give her a little time to cool off. Then maybe he could convince her to forgive him.

Carter didn't want to consider the alternative. The thought of leaving California without resolving his relationship with Gillian made him feel sick inside.

"Excuse me," said a voice behind him.

He turned around to see a woman he didn't recognize standing in the aisle. "Yes?"

"Are these the horses from Quest Stables?"

He studied the woman as he stripped off his gloves, hoping she wasn't another reporter looking for a new angle on the scandal. She appeared to be in her late thirties, with a California tan and dark brown eyes.

"Yes, they are." He stepped out of the stall. "Can I help you with something?"

She held out one hand. "My name is Amanda Emory. Jenna Preston just hired me as the new office manager for Quest Stables."

"I'm Carter Phillips, head veterinarian." He shook her hand, more confused than ever. "Why did Jenna send you to Del Mar?"

"She didn't send me here," Amanda clarified. "I live in California and haven't actually started the job yet. My children and I are moving to Kentucky, but we wanted to visit their grandmother in San Diego before we left. I promised the boys we could see some of the Quest horses since we were so close to Del Mar."

Carter looked around, then saw two young boys watching a horse in another stall get a brisk rubdown.

"Kiefer…Max," Amanda called out to them.

Carter watched them turn around and hurry over to her. The oldest looked about nine or ten and the youngest maybe six. They both stuck close to their mother's side while looking shyly at Carter.

"This is Dr. Phillips," Amanda told them. "He's the veterinarian at Quest."

Kiefer's eyes widened. "They have their own veterinarian?"

Carter found himself smiling for the first time since Gillian had confronted him with the letter from the DNA lab. "More than one, but I'm in charge."

"That's cool," the boy exclaimed.

Carter glanced at his watch. "If you stick around, you can meet some of the trainers and even a jockey."

Kiefer turned to Amanda. "Can we stay, Mom? Please?"

Amanda shook her head. "I'm sorry, but we have to leave. I told you this would be a quick trip. Grandma has reservations to take us all out to eat."

"Don't worry," Carter said when he saw the boy's crestfallen expression. "You'll be able to meet them in Kentucky."

His face brightened. "Cool."

The other little boy worked up enough courage to take a couple of steps toward him and whisper something.

Carter knelt down so he could hear him better. "Can you say that again?"

"I like horses," he whispered.

"Then, you're going to love Kentucky, because it's full of horses."

"Cool," he replied, imitating his big brother.

Amanda smiled at him as he straightened to his full height. "It was nice meeting you, Dr. Phillips."

"Same here. I hope you have a good trip tomorrow."

"Me, too," she said, then corralled her children and headed for the door.

Carter watched them leave. Before he'd met Gillian, he hadn't thought much about having a family of his own. The fact that he was even considering the possibility showed him what an impact she'd had on his life in the short time he'd known her.

He could picture a little girl with Gillian's dark hair and artistic talent. Or a boy with his stubbornness and her green eyes. Carter could teach them about horses and...

He shook that fantasy from his head. Gillian didn't even want to talk to him at the moment, much less have his children. Besides, she was too young for him, and even if they overcame that obstacle there were others standing in their way. Carter didn't want to add to the turmoil in her life, but he didn't know if he could walk away. The only thing he knew for certain was that his life would never be the same.

Gillian might have driven around for hours if she hadn't remembered Jon's offer to let her paint in his backroom studio at the Arcano Gallery. She didn't want to go home and face Herman, not yet certain what she should say to him, if anything. She didn't want to go to Del Mar either, where she risked running into Carter. Yet, she needed to sketch or paint or do something to help release this tension that threatened to overwhelm her.

She pulled her car into the back alley, then parked in one of the spaces behind the gallery. Walking around to the front of the building, she met Amy, Jon's young intern, at the door.

"Hi there," Amy said. "I was just leaving."

"Jon told me I could use his studio to paint," Gillian informed her. "Are you going to be gone long?"

"All afternoon." Amy grimaced. "Root canal."

"Oh, I'm sorry."

Amy peered through the glass door of the studio. "Jon's not here yet, but I don't think he'd mind if I let you in."

"That would be great."

Gillian watched her dig a set of keys out of her small purse. Amy inserted one of them into the door, then turned the latch. "Just make sure you lock the door so no one disturbs you. The gallery doesn't officially open for a few more hours."

"Thanks." Gillian opened the door and walked inside. "Good luck with your root canal."

Amy waved to her, then headed down the sidewalk.

Gillian locked the door behind her, anxious to start sketching something. She found it a little strange that none of her art was on the walls yet, but she walked straight to the back studio, too upset to worry about it.

Setting a blank canvas on one of the easels, she picked up a piece of charcoal and began to sketch. She didn't take time to consider what she wanted to draw, though it soon became apparent. With just a few quick strokes, Carter's face began to appear.

She'd drawn him before, right after they'd met, but this was different. Her sketch had more depth now. She'd seen the way the color of his eyes changed when he looked at her with desire. How his mouth curved up when he smiled.

Her hand didn't stop moving as she rubbed the charcoal across the canvas, filling in the tiny details that she'd learned while lying naked in his arms. Gillian didn't want to think about never being there again or, worse, being replaced by another woman.

Carter was a handsome, virile man. The women back in Kentucky probably fell over themselves trying to catch his attention.

She dropped her hand and stepped back, looking at the man who had almost broken her heart. *Almost.* Because what she saw in the picture she'd just drawn was a man who had love in his eyes.

Love for her.

She'd seen it last night when he'd made love to her. Even this morning, when she'd practically thrown that envelope in his face, Carter's eyes had told her the truth. He loved her. She knew he did.

Yet, he'd betrayed her.

She set the charcoal down, then picked up a towel and wiped her hands clean. Carter had claimed he'd ordered the test to protect her. She wished now that he'd done a better job of explaining what he meant.

Everything she knew about him up until this point told her he was a man who protected others. He watched out for his parents and his wayward brother. Noah had called him the perfect son and Carter had confessed to her how he'd given up his dream of teaching so he could earn enough money to support his parents.

Gillian began to stroll aimlessly around the studio, lost in her thoughts. She'd told Carter that she was tired of secrets and lies, but hadn't she been lying to herself? Refusing to allow a blood test for Picture of Perfection was a form of lying.

If she hadn't been afraid that there might be a connection between Leopold's Legacy and Picture of Perfection, she wouldn't have refused the test. Even if he did win the Pacific Classic, she'd always wonder....

Gillian shook that thought from her head, too confused to think about it anymore. If she wasn't due to meet Jon in an hour, she might even take Carter up on his offer to sit down and talk about it.

As she walked around the studio, she looked for things to do to make that hour go faster. Gillian wiped down the counters and found several bristle brushes that had dried paint in them. She filled a can with paint thinner and dropped the brushes in to soak. Cleaning up a little was the least she could do to repay Jon for displaying her work and giving her a place to decompress.

He had several canvases stacked along one wall and she began to thumb through them, noting that some of them were quite old. It was interesting to see how his technique had changed over the years. His early work was interesting, with several portraits of homeless men that incorporated the same dark elements that she'd observed in his paintings of the cavern. What she found most fascinating was that he didn't have any portraits of women.

Except one.

Gillian stared at the portrait and felt her blood turn to ice in her veins. It was a portrait of her mother wearing her favorite dress.

The front door of the gallery opened and she heard footsteps heading toward her. She turned around to see Jon enter the studio. Something about his face seemed different. Familiar. She realized now that it was a face she'd seen before a long time ago.

A face in a window.

Eighteen

The border collie announced Carter's arrival at Robards Farm by running ahead of his car and barking loudly. A few moments later, the front door of the house opened and Herman stepped out onto the porch.

Carter muttered an oath as he parked the car and cut the engine. Herman's return practically guaranteed that Gillian wasn't here. He'd given up trying to call her, preferring to make his apology in person. Even if she didn't accept it, he intended to make his feelings for her perfectly clear.

Herman climbed down from the porch as Carter exited his car. The border collie pranced around Herman's ankles, his tail wagging.

"Looks like Ranger's foot is better."

Herman nodded. "It sure is. Thanks to you and that salve."

Carter glanced at the house. "Is Gillian here?"

Herman shook his head. "I haven't seen her, but I just got back about an hour ago. Why are you looking for her?"

He noticed that same protective edge in Herman's voice that he'd heard before. It contradicted the slight evidence they'd gleaned from Gillian's therapy sessions that Herman might be the arsonist. At this moment, Carter knew that was ridiculous.

"I messed up," Carter said, finally answering his question. "I ordered a DNA test for Picture of Perfection without Gillian's permission."

Herman scowled. "And you still have the guts to show your face around here?"

Carter didn't blame him for his reaction—he'd expect nothing less from a man who had taken care of her for the last twelve years. "I'm here because I love Gillian and she means more to me than a DNA test or anything else. She needs to know that, just like she needs you to stop lying to her."

A hard glint shone in Herman's eyes. "What's that supposed to mean?"

"You not only lied to her about the cause of the fire, but about your relationship with her mother." Now that Carter had gone this far he didn't intend to stop. Gillian couldn't keep living in limbo. She was so confused about the past that she couldn't move forward into the future.

Herman paled at his words. "Gillian knows about that?"

Carter nodded. "She's known for years. She found the love letter her mother wrote to you, but she couldn't bring herself to ask you about it."

The older man walked over to the porch and slumped down on one of the steps. "I guess you're not the only one who messed up."

The border collie stood near Herman, his tail still wagging, but the man didn't appear to see him. "It was all so long ago—about two years before the fire. I was a bachelor then and spent a lot of time at the Cameron ranch."

Carter could see the pain in Herman's eyes as he began the story, but he knew it had to be told. He just hoped it wouldn't leave Gillian estranged from the godfather she loved so much.

"The Camerons had been having some rocky times," Herman continued, "both in their marriage and financially. Mark Cameron ended up taking a job that kept him on the road most every week."

Herman looked up at Carter. "Cara Cameron was a beautiful woman and I admit I enjoyed flirting with her. I think she was just lonely and worried that her husband didn't find her attractive anymore. The only thing I can say in our defense is that we never became intimate."

"Did Gillian's father find out about it?"

"No." Herman stretched one leg in front of him. "Cara reconciled with her husband about the same time that I met Marie, so our relationship just kind of fizzled out."

"Then what were you and Mark Cameron fighting about on the day of the fire?"

Herman squinted up at him. "How the hell do you know about that?"

"Gillian saw you. The memory has been buried all these years, but she recovered it during her session with the hypnotist."

"Well, I don't..." His voice trailed off as he started putting it all together. The look of horror on his face convinced Carter of the man's innocence before he spoke again. "My God, Gillian doesn't think I started the fire, does she?"

"She doesn't want to believe it," Carter assured him, "but she still has too many questions about that night. She witnessed you arguing with her father, then later saw a man's face in the window. The memory of that face was too fuzzy for her to identify."

Herman buried his face in his hands. "I never wanted this to happen. I never wanted her to know..."

"Know what?" Carter asked, sensing he was getting closer to the truth. He just wished Gillian was here to hear it.

Herman raised his head. "I did argue with Mark that afternoon, because I didn't think he was taking Cara's stalker seriously."

Carter blinked. "Gillian's mother had a stalker?"

Herman nodded. "She'd hired him to paint a portrait of her as a surprise for Mark. She even pawned some jewelry so she could afford it. But the artist was a lunatic. He wouldn't leave her alone."

"How did you know about it?" Carter asked. "I thought your relationship with her had ended."

"It had," Herman confirmed. "Cara was happy with Mark and I was in love with Marie. After we married, the two women became friends, even though I'd told Marie about what had happened between us."

"She must have been a remarkable woman."

Love and pain shone in his eyes. "She was. I thought I'd die when I lost her."

For the first time in his life, Carter could understand that kind of love. "So Cara told your wife about the stalker?"

Herman nodded, then took a deep breath to gather himself. "Cara was afraid of him. That's what I was trying to make clear to Mark that afternoon, because he wasn't taking it very seriously. I think I must have gotten through to him, though, because he stayed home that night instead of leaving on his business trip."

"But why would this stalker set fire to the house when he knew Gillian's mother was in it?"

Herman shrugged. "I guess that's something we'll never know. By the time the fire department determined it was arson, the guy was gone."

"Was he questioned after the fire?"

Herman shook his head. "No one could locate him. It was like he just vanished." The older man looked at Carter. "That's the reason I never told Gillian about him."

"I don't understand."

Herman stood up and walked a few paces, his gaze on the horizon. Then he turned around to face Carter. "My mother was attacked by a stranger when I was eight years old. I saw the way it changed her. The man was never caught and she always feared he'd come back and hurt her again."

Carter could see the gleam of tears in Herman's eyes. "You were afraid Gillian would react the same way."

He nodded. "My mother went from being a happy, carefree woman to one who refused to ever leave our house. She let her fear of that stranger destroy the rest of her life."

Now Carter understood why Herman had been so reluctant for Gillian to open that door to her past. He'd been afraid of losing his goddaughter just as he'd lost his mother—not physically, but emotionally.

"You have to tell her the truth," Carter said, knowing it shouldn't come from him.

"I suppose you're right." Herman heaved a deep sigh. "I just hope Gillian can handle it."

"She can," Carter said firmly. "Gillian's a strong, beautiful, talented woman. Look how much she's come through already and what she's accomplished. I think she's amazing."

Herman's eyes widened, then a slow smile spread

across his face. "That's quite a speech, Carter. So why the hell are you telling it to me instead of her?"

He kicked a pebble in frustration. "Because I can't find her. Gillian disappeared as soon as she learned about the DNA test."

Herman glanced at his watch. "Seems like I saw something on her calendar about a meeting at the Arcano Gallery. Maybe that's where she is."

Carter moved toward his car, wondering why he hadn't thought of that himself, especially with her opening debut scheduled for Friday."

"Hey, Carter," Herman called after him.

He opened the car door, eager to be on his way. "Yeah?"

"I think you should pick up some flowers. Marie loved roses, so I always bought her a dozen or so whenever I did something stupid."

Carter looked at him. "It almost sounds like you're on my side."

"I'm on Gillian's side," Herman said evenly. "And I'm starting to believe you might be the right man for her after all. I just hope it's not too late to convince her."

A prickle of fear ran up Gillian's spine as Jon walked over to her.

"What are you doing?" he asked.

Her mouth went dry. "Nothing."

His gaze moved to the portrait of her mother. "Do you like it?"

Gillian didn't know what to say. She remembered him now. Jon was the artist who had painted her mother all those years ago. Although, he'd called himself something different then.

"No, really," Jon entreated, taking her silence as shyness. "I'd appreciate the opinion of a fellow artist. The subject is beautiful." His fingers brushed over the canvas, touching her mother's face like a caress. "You can see the love my dear Cara has shining in her eyes. Love for me."

"No," Gillian blurted. "That's not true!"

Jon slowly turned to her. "How would you know? You were just a child. She wanted me just as I wanted her."

Nausea welled up in her stomach and Gillian thought she might be sick. "She loved my father."

Anger contorted his face. "Your father killed her!"

She shook her head. "No…"

"Yes," Jon insisted. "He wasn't supposed to be home that night. I was going to save her. To make my dear Cara finally realize that I was the only man she could ever depend on. Then I saw him carry you up the stairs and came up with an even better plan. I'd rescue her and let the two of you die in the fire. Then I could have my love all to myself."

Gillian took a step away from him, the horror of the night rushing back to her. But there was no escape. Jon blocked her path to the door and the memories that had eluded her for so long now threatened to overwhelm her.

"There was so much smoke," Jon said softly, his mind in another place. "I tried to make it to Cara's room, but I couldn't breathe."

Gillian could still feel the terror that had pounded inside of her as she'd tried to escape the burning house. She had crawled down the hallway, clinging to Morris as the smoke filled her lungs.

"It was you," she whispered, meeting his gaze. Looking at the man who had haunted her subconscious for so many years. "The man I saw at the end of the hall."

"Yes," Jon affirmed. "I thought it was Cara at first and I was so happy. You both have the same dark hair, but I soon realized my mistake. By then it was too late. There was too much smoke and I could hear someone shouting outside."

Her hands curled into fists as she thought of everything this man had taken from her. She'd not only lost her parents, but her home and her history. She had no other family on either side, so all of her precious mementos had been lost in the flames.

He turned back to the portrait, touching her mother's face once more. "I tried, my love. I tried."

Gillian suppressed a shiver at the depth of his delusions. As an artist, he'd been able to hide them better than other people, since artists were supposed to be a bit eccentric. Now she understood the dark elements in all his paintings—they came from his empty soul.

"I thought Cara was gone forever." Jon smiled. "I changed my name and tried to forget her. Then I saw you at that art symposium last March and knew I'd been given a second chance."

His tone of voice, even more than his words, terrified her. Gillian knew she was treading on dangerous ground. The man had now made her part of his delusions. "Is that why you offered to give me a gallery showing?"

"I had to find a way to get close to you." He walked over to another easel, this one covered with a cloth.

She watched as he pulled the cloth from the canvas, then gasped at what she saw in front of her. It was a picture of Gillian wearing the same blue dress her mother had worn in her portrait.

"Now I know that I wasn't meant to be with Cara, but with you," Jon intoned. "Fate stepped in to save you for me."

"It wasn't fate," she countered, taking a step back from the disturbing portrait in front of her. "It was Ian. He saved me that night while you ran away. You let my parents die while you ran like a coward."

Anger sparked in his eyes. "Don't talk like that to me, Gillian. I am your mentor. Your love. Once we're away from here, you'll see that I did the right thing that night."

A sound from the front of the gallery made them both turn toward the passageway. Gillian could hear someone unlocking the front door and relief flooded through her. By some miracle, Amy had returned.

"If you say or do anything," Jon warned, moving his

suit coat just far enough for her to see a gun protruding from his waistband, "I'll kill her."

Gillian knew he was serious. She gave a slow nod, fear for the young intern flooding through her. Jon brushed past her and walked through the passageway that led to the front of the building. Their voices carried loud enough that Gillian could hear the conversation.

"I thought you had a dentist appointment," Jon said.

"He got sick," Amy exclaimed. "Can you believe it? I was never so happy in my life."

"That is good news."

Gillian was amazed at how sane he sounded now. She looked around the room for a phone, kicking herself for leaving her cell phone in her car. She hadn't wanted any distractions while she painted, not realizing the danger that awaited her.

"You should be out celebrating instead of stuck at work," Jon continued. "Why don't you take the rest of the day off?"

"Seriously?"

Gillian closed her eyes, willing Amy to take him up on his offer. The intern had no idea what kind of man he was or what danger she faced at this moment.

"Absolutely," Jon replied. "I'll be here until late tonight anyway, so I can handle any customers that come in."

"Well, all right," Amy said tentatively. "If you're sure." Then she paused. "Is Ms. Cameron still here? She stopped by earlier to use your studio."

Gillian held her breath, waiting to hear Jon's reaction to the question.

"She must have stepped out for a while," Jon replied. "I noticed her car is still parked out back."

"Okay, well, I guess I'll see you tomorrow." The front door opened.

"Goodbye, Amy."

The door closed again and she heard the sound of a lock being turned. She was well and truly trapped. Knowing she didn't have a moment to spare, Gillian looked around the studio for some kind of weapon she could use to defend herself.

The one thing she knew for certain was that she couldn't let him take her away from here. Then no one would ever find her. She thought about Carter and wished she'd told him that she loved him. Now she might never have that chance.

She spied a putty knife on the counter and slipped it into the pocket of her jeans, even knowing it would be no match for a gun. She had to find a way to catch him by surprise, then incapacitate him long enough to make her escape.

"Sorry about that," Jon said, returning to the back room much too soon.

Gillian leaned against the counter to steady herself, bumping the can of paint thinner with her elbow "That's all right."

She could hear her voice shaking but he seemed oblivious of her fear. Jon carefully placed the drape back over a portrait he'd painted of her. "We'll take this with us. I'll want to do some touch-ups now that I have you with me."

Timing was everything. She needed to make him look at her. "I'm not going with you."

He slowly turned around, his right hand moving toward the gun. Then he started walking toward her. She held her breath, her heart pounding in her chest. When he was only a few steps away from her, she made her move.

Grabbing the can of paint thinner, she splashed the contents in his face, the brushes flying. He screamed as the caustic liquid hit his eyes.

Then she ran for her life.

Nineteen

Carter arrived at the Arcano Gallery only to find the front door locked. He peered through the glass door, hoping to see someone who could tell him what time Gillian was scheduled to meet with the owner. He wasn't going to give up until he found her.

Then he heard a scream.

Gillian.

He tried the door again, then looked frantically around him for something to break the thick glass. Spotting a metal trash can a few feet away, he picked it up and hurled it at the door. The glass shattered and Carter reached inside to unlatch the door.

An alarm sounded, punctuated by another scream.

He looked up to see Gillian appear in the back of the gallery. She looked terrified.

Carter jerked the door open and ran inside to meet her. Then he saw a man burst out of the back passageway.

"Watch out," Gillian warned. "It's Jon. He's got a gun!"

Carter was more worried about her safety than his own. As soon as he saw the deadly weapon in Jon's hand, he pulled Gillian behind him. Jon kept coming at them as he raised the gun and took aim. The man's face was beet-red and his eyes were tearing and bloodshot.

Jon fired at them once, then again. Both shots went wide, his vision obviously impaired. One bullet ricocheted off a tall metal sculpture before landing on the tile floor.

Carter wasn't about to let him get off a third shot. He charged the man, ramming a fist into his gut. Jon doubled over with a loud groan, then Carter punched him with an uppercut to his jaw.

Jon's knees folded under him as he fell to the floor. Gillian walked over to the semiconscious man and kicked the gun out of his hand. It slid several feet across the floor, out of harm's way.

A groan emerged from Jon's mouth as Carter turned him over on his stomach. Then he pulled both of the man's hands behind him. "We need to find something we can use to tie him up."

"Here," Gillian said, moving toward one of the pieces of modern art on display. It was an old rotary telephone sitting on a rusty milk can. She disconnected the phone cord and brought it over to Carter.

Jon lifted his head off the floor as Carter tightly wound the thick vinyl cord around the man's wrists. "That really hurts."

"Good," Carter replied, wishing the man had put up a better fight so he could have hit him a few more times. He gave the final knot a good, hard tug to make sure it was secure, then rose to his feet.

A crowd had gathered outside the broken glass door.

"Hey," somebody shouted, "is this performance art?"

Carter turned away from them to find a pale Gillian standing right behind him.

"You came for me," she said hoarsely.

Carter pulled her into his arms and swore to himself that he'd never let her go again. "Are you all right?"

She didn't say anything for a long moment and he could feel her body shaking. "Well, I guess my gallery debut is canceled. Other than that, I think I'm okay."

It was a weak attempt at humor and he was amazed she could even joke about it. He could also tell she was in shock.

He walked her farther away from the crowd, wanting to get her away from any unnecessary commotion. Her attacker was rolling around on the floor, moaning in pain.

"What happened to his face?" Carter asked as he saw the angry red blotches that had started to emerge on the man's cheeks and chin.

Even though it was seventy-five degrees outside, Gillian wrapped her arms around herself as if she was cold. "I threw paint thinner at him to get away."

"Smart thinking," Carter said, constantly impressed with her fortitude.

"I didn't think I was going to make it." She looked up at Carter. "Then I saw you."

He didn't want to consider what might have happened if he'd given up searching for her. He saw her hands shaking and reached out to clasp them in his own. Her fingers were ice-cold. "Did he hurt you?"

She shook her head. "No, but I remember everything now. He's the man I saw in the window that night. He started the fire that killed my parents."

"You're sure?"

She nodded. "He didn't even try to deny it."

"How did he get away with it for so long?" Carter muttered.

"He must have changed his name and started over. He's crazy, Carter. He has no conscience. No soul. He was obsessed with my mother and thought I was his second chance at love."

That just made Carter want to hit him again. Instead, he pulled Gillian into his arms, so grateful that she was safe from that mad man.

"I think he's the reason I've been having those nightmares," Gillian said, lifting her head to look at him. "They started right around the time I met him at that art symposium in San Francisco."

"After you saw him, you started having nightmares, even though your conscious mind didn't recognize him."

"Strange, isn't it," she murmured. "The nightmares were like a warning for me. Without my memories to guide me, my subconscious took over like some kind of internal security system."

A siren sounded in the distance. "It's over now," Carter told her. "He won't ever be able to hurt anyone again."

She closed her eyes. "I'm so relieved that Herman wasn't the arsonist. I feel so guilty for even suspecting that he might have been involved."

"Herman feels guilty, too," Carter said gently. "He wants to explain why he kept so many things from you. In his own way, I think Herman really was trying to protect you."

The sirens grew louder and Carter glanced over his shoulder to see three patrol cars pull up in front of the gallery. He knew he didn't have much time before the police interrupted them.

He needed to tell Gillian he loved her. If she didn't believe anything else he told her, he wanted her to believe that.

"Gillian," he began, turning around just in time to see her eyes roll back in her head. He caught her just before she hit the floor.

* * *

"Where is Gillian?" Carter demanded as he sat in a small room at the police station. "I have to see her."

"She's fine." Detective Kovacs was an older woman with short gray hair and pale blue eyes. "According to the doctor in the emergency room, she simply fainted. Probably due to the stress of the incident and the fact that she hadn't eaten all day."

Carter leaned back against the chair and breathed a sigh of relief. He still couldn't believe they'd arrested him along with Jon Castello. Then again, the crowd gathered at the gallery had given different reports about what happened. Some had even accused Carter of having the gun first.

"When can I see her?" he asked.

"I'm afraid she's not here." Detective Kovacs turned a page in her notebook. She sat across the table from him, a pair of bifocals perched on her nose. She'd been taking notes while he'd given his statement.

He leaned forward. "Where is she?"

She peered at him from over her bifocals. "We allowed Ms. Cameron to give her statement at the hospital, then she was allowed to go home. I believe her godfather picked her up."

Carter knew she was in good hands with Herman, but that didn't make him any less anxious to see her. He leaned his forearms on the table, wondering how much longer this was all going to take.

At least he'd had a chance to call Marcus on the way

to the police station and explain why he wasn't at the racetrack. The head trainer for Quest Stables had been shocked at the story and had encouraged Carter to take all the time he needed.

"So the gun belonged to Mr. Castello?" the detective asked.

"Yes," he replied, wondering how many times he'd have to repeat this story. He wasn't worried about facing charges. Once they compared his statement with Gillian's, they'd see that Jon Castello was responsible for all of this. Hell, once they talked to the man, they'd have no doubt about it.

"He fired two shots?"

Carter nodded. "Yes, right before I hit him."

She arched a brow. "You broke three of his ribs."

"Is that all?" Carter asked, feeling very little sympathy for the man. Whether or not Jon Castello was legally responsible for his crimes didn't change the fact that he'd done much more damage to Gillian than a few broken ribs.

A knock sounded at the door and a uniformed officer handed a folder to Detective Kovacs. She laid it on the table in front of her and opened it.

"Well, this is interesting," Detective Kovacs said, adjusting her bifocals. "It seems Jon Castello's real name is Jonah Callow. He's forty years old and is originally from Florida. Looks like he was arrested for a series of Peeping Tom incidents and one assault as a young man."

"Will he be charged with the crime he committed twelve years ago?"

She nodded. "There's no statute of limitations for either arson or murder in the state of California. He confessed to it when we brought him in, so now it will be up to the lawyers to sort it all out."

As long as the man was out of Gillian's life, Carter didn't care what happened to him. "Is there anything else you need from me?"

She closed the file in front of her. "I think that will do for now. It looks like you acted in self-defense when you hit Mr. Castello. We've got your cell phone number and your telephone number in Kentucky if we need to reach you, but I really doubt that will be necessary."

"Thank you," Carter rose to his feet. "Can I go now?"

"Of course." Detective Kovacs stood up to open the door for him. "Have a nice life, Dr. Phillips."

That was his plan. As he left the police station, Carter reached for his cell phone to call Andrew Preston. He was ready to make some changes.

Twenty

Gillian stood in the gazebo that evening, watching her horses grazing in the lush green pasture. It seemed strange that only a few short hours ago a madman was holding her at gunpoint. Peace and solitude surrounded her now, something she'd sought for so long. That wasn't enough for her anymore. She was finally ready to put her past behind her and move on.

Ready to follow her heart.

"Herman told me I could find you here." Carter stepped into the gazebo.

Gillian's skin tingled at the sound of his voice. She set down the artist's brush in her hand, then turned around to face him. "What took you so long?"

He gave her a wry smile. "To tell you the truth, I wasn't sure you'd want to see me." Then his smile faded as he pulled a crumpled envelope out of his pocket. "Here you go."

She took it from him. "What's this?"

"The DNA test results. I haven't opened them because they don't belong to me." He moved a step closer to her. "I never should have ordered that test, Gillian. It was your call to make, and no matter how I tried to rationalize it, I was still wrong."

She looked up at him. "What do you want me to do with it?"

He shrugged his broad shoulders. "I don't care. Throw it away or rip it to pieces. Whatever you want as long as it doesn't come between us anymore."

"I have a better idea," she said, then broke the seal with her index finger and pulled out the sheet of paper inside.

His eyes widened in surprise. "What are you doing?"

"Something I should have done the first time you asked me. If Picture of Perfection isn't sired by Apollo's Ice then I want to know before he races in the Pacific Classic. I *need* to know."

She sucked in a deep breath as she looked at the paper, knowing that whatever it said could have a significant impact on her life. Only she found herself staring at an incomprehensible series of numbers. After all the turmoil she'd been through about this test, Gillian couldn't help but laugh.

"You take it," she said, handing it to Carter. "I have no idea what any of this means."

His brow furrowed as he took the paper from her to study the test results.

"Well?" she prodded, eager to know the answer.

He looked up at her, relief washing over his face. "Apollo's Ice *is* the sire of Picture of Perfection."

"Are you sure?"

"Positive." Carter stuffed the paper back into the envelope. "I've studied the DNA chart for Apollo's Ice so many times that I've got it memorized. You don't have anything to worry about now, Gillian. As strange as it seems, given their identical coloring, there's no connection between Picture of Perfection and Leopold's Legacy."

"You don't seem too upset about it," she said, confused by his reaction.

"Upset? I'm thrilled. The last thing I wanted to do was destroy your dreams." Carter reached out to caress the hollow of her cheek. "I love you, Gillian Cameron. I only want you to be happy."

"Then kiss me," she said, stepping into his arms. "Because I love you and I can't imagine ever being happy without you in my life."

He braced his hands on her hips and pulled her tight against him. "If I start kissing you, I'm not sure I'll be able to stop."

"Is that supposed to be some kind of threat?" she asked, relishing the way her body fit so perfectly against him.

"Take it any way you want," he replied, then he kissed her with a passion that literally lifted her off her feet.

"And it's Jack Be Nimble in the lead with Gift of Gold running on the outside. Picture of Perfection is coming up strong at the first turn."

It was a beautiful summer afternoon at the Del Mar racetrack and the Pacific Classic was in full swing. Carter turned to watch Gillian's reaction as the announcer called the race over the loud speaker.

"Come on, Picture of Perfection," she shouted as she leaned out over the white railing in their box. "You can do it! Go, baby, go!"

He smiled at her enthusiasm, just as he had when she'd awakened him in bed this morning to make love. That's when he'd learned that her creativity wasn't just limited to her artistic endeavors.

"Now it's Gift of Gold taking the lead by a head with Jack Be Nimble in second and Picture of Perfection holding his own in third. The rest of the field is fading with a large gap of six to seven lengths."

Gillian grasped his arm. "Look, Carter, I think he's gaining! He's going to do it!"

Carter circled his arm around her waist as he watched jockey Finn Wiley start to make his move. "Come on, Picture of Perfection!"

"They're racing down the backstretch and Picture of Perfection is starting to turn on the heat. Picture of Perfection has moved into second, passing Jack Be

Nimble and coming up hard on Gift of Gold as they head into the turn."

"Go, Picture of Perfection!" Gillian cried, jumping up and down.

Herman stood on the other side of her with his date, Shirley Biden. Gillian had suggested he invite the kind woman she'd met at the Turf Club Ball and the two of them seemed to be hitting it off. They were both excited about the race, Shirley's bag of popcorn flying into the air as she cheered Gillian's horse on.

Carter's heart began to pound as the horses headed for the finish line. He'd been to more horse races than he could count, but had never been this nervous about the outcome before.

"Gift of Gold and Picture of Perfection are neck and neck with Jack Be Nimble now behind by a length. Gift of Gold pulls ahead by a nose…now it's Picture of Perfection. Here comes Gift of Gold again and we're coming down by the wire. And Picture of Perfection surges ahead. Picture of Perfection wins the Pacific Classic!"

Gillian screamed and leaped into Carter's arms. He spun her around, lifting his face to the sky and shouting with joy.

"He did it," Gillian exclaimed. "Picture of Perfection actually did it!"

"You'll be even more famous now," Carter teased her.

News about the incident at the Arcano Gallery had generated all kinds of publicity for Gillian's portraits.

She was getting rave reviews from art critics and had several hefty commissions already lined up for the next year.

"I don't care about being famous," she said as he lowered her to the ground. "I just want to be happy."

"Then I hope this makes you happy." Carter reached into his pocket and pulled out a small, blue velvet box. He'd intended to give it to her in private, without thousands of people surrounding them, but now just seemed like the perfect moment.

"Oh, Carter," she whispered, taking the box from him.

He saw Herman give him a thumbs-up as he and Shirley quietly left the box. Then he turned his attention back to the woman he loved.

She slowly lifted the lid, then gasped when she saw the antique topaz ring nestled inside. Tears filled her eyes as she looked up at him. "It's the most beautiful ring I've ever seen."

"Then you like it?"

"Like it?" she asked incredulously. "I love it and I love you. Does this mean...?"

He grinned, amazed he'd been able to keep the news to himself for this long. "Well, it's not official yet, but I'm interviewing for a job as an associate professor of equine medicine at the University of California here in San Diego."

Her green eyes widened. "Carter, are you serious?

You're going to move here. You're going to be a college professor?"

"I hope so," he replied. "I've talked with the head of the veterinary department at the university and he seems impressed by my résumé. It may take some time to work out all the details, but I feel pretty confident."

"What about Quest?"

"I've been talking with Andrew Preston about it. If I take the job here in California, he wants me to stay on at Quest as a consultant. We've still got a mystery to solve and I'm not one to give up easily. Plus, I'll still travel the racing circuit with them during the summer break."

"That's wonderful!"

He nodded. "I finally figured out a way to follow my dream and take care of my parents. By the way, I told them all about you and they can't wait to meet you."

She smiled. "I hope I'm good enough for their perfect son."

He laughed. "I'm far from perfect."

"But our love is perfect," she told him, leaning in for another kiss, "and that's all we'll ever need."

* * * * *

Rufus, as Crystal Hayes had decided to call the black Lab, slept soundly on the soft seat even as she maneuvered the Softco truck in front of the Dean Grosso garage. Engines fired through the open bay doors, compressors clacked and impact tools whined as the teams tweaked their race cars in preparation for qualifying at the third race in Charlotte.

As always when she visited the garage area, Crystal experienced a vicarious thrill, watching the technicians' meticulous, last-minute preparations. As the daughter of a machinist, she understood the difference a fraction of a degree or a thousandth of an inch could make in the performance of a race car.

She muscled the driver's door shut behind her and waved hello to a couple of familiar crew members in their white-and-pale-blue jump suits. Then she rounded the back of the truck and rolled up the door. Inside, five boxes were marked Cargill Motors.

One of them was big and heavy, and it had slid forward a few feet, probably when she'd braked to make the narrow parking lot entrance. So she pushed up the sleeves of her canary-yellow T-shirt, then stretched forward to reach the box. A couple of catcalls came her way as her faded blue jeans tightened across her rear end. But she knew they were good-natured, and she simply ignored them.

She dragged the box toward her over the gritty metal floor.

"Let me give you a hand with that," a deep, melodious voice rumbled in her ear.

"I can manage," she responded crisply, not wanting to engage with any of the catcallers.

Here in the garage, the last thing she needed was one of the guys treating her as if she was something other than, well, one of the guys.

She'd learned long ago there was something about her that made men toss out pickup lines like parade candy. And she'd been around race crews long enough to know she needed to behave like a buddy, not a potential date.

She piled the smaller boxes on top of the large one.

"It looks heavy," said the voice.

"I'm tough," she assured him as she scooped the pile into her arms.

He didn't move away, so she turned her head to subject him to a *back off* stare. But she found herself staring into a compelling pair of green…no, brown…no, hazel eyes. She did a double take as they seemed to twinkle, multicolored, under the garage lights.

The man insistently held out his hands for the boxes. There was a dignity in his tone and little crinkles around his eyes that hinted at wisdom. There wasn't a single sign of flirtation in his expression, but Crystal was still cautious.

"You know I'm being paid to move this, right?" she asked him.

"That doesn't mean I can't be a gentleman."

Somebody whistled from a workbench. "Go, Professor Larry."

The man named Larry tossed a "Back off" over his shoulder. Then he turned to Crystal. "Sorry about that."

"Are you for real?" she asked, growing uncomfortable with the attention they were drawing. The last thing she needed was some latter-day Sir Galahad defending her honor at the track.

He quirked a dark eyebrow in a question.

"I mean," she elaborated, "you don't need to worry. I've been fending off the wolves since I was seventeen."

"Doesn't make it right," he countered, attempting to lift the boxes from her hands.

She jerked back. "You're not making it any easier."
He frowned.

"You carry this box, and they start thinking of me as a girl."

Professor Larry dipped his gaze to take in the curves of her figure. "Hate to tell you this," he said, a little twinkle coming into those multifaceted eyes.

Something about his look made her shiver inside. It was a ridiculous reaction. Guys had given her the once-over a million times. She'd learned long ago to ignore it.

"Odds are," Larry continued, a teasing drawl in his tone, "they already have."

She turned pointedly away, boxes in hand as she marched across the floor. She could feel him watching her from behind.

* * * * *

*Crystal Hayes could do without her looks,
men obsessed with her looks, and guys who think
they're God's gift to the ladies.
Would Larry be the one guy who could blow all
of Crystal's preconceptions away?
Look for OVERHEATED
by Barbara Dunlop.
On sale July 29, 2008.*

Harlequin® Historical
Historical Romantic Adventure!

From *USA TODAY*
bestselling author

Margaret Moore

A LOVER'S KISS

A Frenchwoman in London,
Juliette Bergerine is unexpectedly
thrown together in hiding with
Sir Douglas Drury. As lust and
desire give way to deeper emotions,
how will Juliette react on discovering
that her brother was murdered—
by Drury!

*Available September
wherever you buy books.*

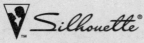

Silhouette®

Romantic
SUSPENSE

**Sparked by Danger,
Fueled by Passion.**

Cindy Dees
Killer Affair

Seduction in the sand...and a killer on the beach.

Can-do girl Madeline Crummby is off to a remote
Fijian island to review an exclusive resort, and she hires
Tom Laruso, a burned-out bodyguard, to fly her there
in spite of an approaching hurricane. When their plane
crashes, they are trapped on an island with a serial killer
who stalks overaffectionate couples. When their false
attempts to lure out the killer turn all too real, Tom and
Madeline must risk their lives and their hearts....

**Look for the third installment
of this thrilling miniseries,
available August 2008
wherever books are sold.**

REQUEST YOUR FREE BOOKS!
2 FREE NOVELS PLUS 2 FREE GIFTS!

SPECIAL EDITION®
Life, Love and Family!

YES! Please send me 2 FREE Silhouette Special Edition® novels and my 2 FREE gifts (gifts are worth about $10). After receiving them, if I don't wish to receive any more books, I can return the shipping statement marked "cancel." If I don't cancel, I will receive 6 brand-new novels every month and be billed just $4.24 per book in the U.S. or $4.99 per book in Canada, plus 25¢ shipping and handling per book and applicable taxes, if any*. That's a savings of at least 15% off the cover price! I understand that accepting the 2 free books and gifts places me under no obligation to buy anything. I can always return a shipment and cancel at any time. Even if I never buy another book from Silhouette, the two free books and gifts are mine to keep forever.

235 SDN EEYU   335 SDN EEY6

Name	(PLEASE PRINT)

Address	Apt. #

City	State/Prov.	Zip/Postal Code

Signature (if under 18, a parent or guardian must sign)

Mail to the **Silhouette Reader Service:**
IN U.S.A.: P.O. Box 1867, Buffalo, NY 14240-1867
IN CANADA: P.O. Box 609, Fort Erie, Ontario L2A 5X3

Not valid to current subscribers of Silhouette Special Edition books.

Want to try two free books from another line?
Call 1-800-873-8635 or visit www.morefreebooks.com.

* Terms and prices subject to change without notice. N.Y. residents add applicable sales tax. Canadian residents will be charged applicable provincial taxes and GST. Offer not valid in Quebec. This offer is limited to one order per household. All orders subject to approval. Credit or debit balances in a customer's account(s) may be offset by any other outstanding balance owed by or to the customer. Please allow 4 to 6 weeks for delivery. Offer available while quantities last.

Your Privacy: Silhouette is committed to protecting your privacy. Our Privacy Policy is available online at www.eHarlequin.com or upon request from the Reader Service. From time to time we make our lists of customers available to reputable third parties who may have a product or service of interest to you. If you would prefer we not share your name and address, please check here. ☐

SSE08R

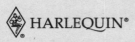

HARLEQUIN®

American ★ Romance®

CATHY MCDAVID
Cowboy Dad
THE STATE OF PARENTHOOD

Natalie Forrester's job at Bear Creek Ranch
is to make everyone welcome, which is an
easy task when it comes to Aaron Reyes—the
unwelcome cowboy and part-owner. His
tenderness toward Natalie's infant daughter
melts the single mother's heart. What's not
so easy to accept is that falling for him means
giving up her job, her family and the only
home she's ever known....

**Available August
wherever books are sold.**

LOVE, HOME & HAPPINESS

www.eHarlequin.com   HAR75225

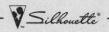

SPECIAL EDITION™

NEW YORK TIMES BESTSELLING AUTHOR

DIANA PALMER

A brand-new Long, Tall Texans novel

HEART OF STONE

Feeling unwanted and unloved, Keely returns
to Jacobsville and to Boone Sinclair, a rancher
troubled by his own past. Boone has always
seemed reserved, but now Keely discovers a
sensuality with him that quickly turns to love. Can
they each see past their own scars to let love in?

*Available September 2008
wherever you buy books.*